From a sleepy village in Bengal, to the fast paced cities of New Delhi, Kolkata, New York and London, in the eleven stories in this collection, Erika Banerji evokes lives and landscapes with delicate care and elegance. An estranged couple discover that illness heals their relationship; a schoolgirl reveals the tragic truth behind the life of her teacher; a maid reconciles to life and marriage back in her village after years of working in the big city; a young Punjabi woman leaves everything behind to marry a stranger in London; a computer salesman secretly wishes for an alternative life in New York and Hiren Mukherjee reluctantly retires to a life which he had not expected for himself. These are moving and subtle tales which explore the significance of the understated moments in the lives of men and women confined to their worlds of domestic unease. Brimming with sharp observations of lives in the East as well as the West *Amongst Other Things* reflects the author's infinite sympathy for the otherwise ordinary.

ERIKA BANERJI was born in Assam and educated in New Delhi and London. Her prizewinning stories have appeared in a number of literary journals including *Wasafiri* and *MsLexia*. *Amongst Other Things* is her first published collection. She lives in London.

Erika Banerji

Amongst Other Things

— **Stories** —

ISBN: 978-1-4834-1135-4 (sc)
ISBN: 978-1-4834-1136-1 (e)

Lulu Publishing Services rev. date: 05/27/2014

For my Ahana and Aaryaman

Contents

Mrs Luthra's Stove

I first learnt about the custom of dowry from my Hindi teacher. It was not really the kind of knowledge she should have been sharing with a nine-year-old girl, but I think that it was a matter which had preoccupied her lately and it made her want to bring it up in our conversations. Her name was Deepika Puri and she had joined my school, which was a private school in an affluent Delhi neighbourhood soon after completing her B Ed degree. When she joined she couldn't have been older than twenty-two or twenty-three and was slim and petite and rather reticent with her pupils.

A year after she started, news spread that she was soon to be married. This information was cause for a lot of excitement and speculation amongst us young girls. In the past we had observed in our teachers the curious transformations brought about by marriage. Now we nervously anticipated the same changes, which would inevitably overcome the demure Miss Puri.

In the days leading up to the wedding there was something melancholy about the otherwise pleasant Miss Puri. She was more than usually withdrawn. At school she was by now well liked by most of the other teachers and yet we often saw her sitting in the staff common room by herself, staring out of the windows, which looked onto the playground where we spent our breaks. I remember how at the beginning of the school year she was quite lenient in her methods. She rarely surprised us with tests, and unlike most other teachers she always gave us an extra mark when in doubt about an answer. She smiled a lot in those days, and although not outwardly gregarious, distinctly enjoyed the effusiveness of those of us in class who were.

When rumour of her marriage went around the school she would come to class with a distracted air about herself. Sometimes she would suggest we read a few pages out of our textbooks to ourselves and she would sit at her desk scribbling onto a piece of paper. She barely noticed us anymore, and if she did it was only to shout a command, it was almost as if an automaton had replaced her, but we girls, excited as we were about the thought of her getting married put it down to wedding nerves. It is only now, as I think back that these details come back to me and I realize how much, in the days leading up to and after her marriage she changed from being an endearing gentle teacher to an aloof stentorian.

In those days our own adolescent ideas of marriage were clouded in a romantic haze. We imagined our teacher putting together her trousseau, and we often spent hours discussing what shade of red she should wear as her wedding sari, whether on the day her hair should be piled on top of her head or left loose around her shoulders? Questions we asked and answered ourselves, eager to create a picture in our young minds of the always blissfully happy bride-to-be. We found out from whispers that leaked steadily out of the staffroom like a zealous serpent, that she was marrying a businessman who lived in West Delhi. We hoped in our young hearts that we would have the good fortune to catch a glimpse of the groom before the wedding, but we were never encouraged to ask our teacher questions, and she never shared any pictures or information with the class.

A fortnight after the wedding Miss Puri returned to school as Mrs Luthra. The change began with her name but we were quite taken aback by the extent of the physical transformation that had by then begun to take place in our once mild and modest teacher. To begin with she seemed so much more impatient with us, her voice, once so pleasant and hushed had found itself a new octave much higher than before. As is customary with married women in North India her hands and arms were stained with the delicate pattern of *mehndi*. The flowers and leaves inched up from her fingertips to her elbows, like the greedy vine of some stealthy bloodsucking plant. Her wrists were also adorned with a jangling set of wedding bangles or *chuddha* as they were called, ivory and red, the mark of the married woman. She also wore the most inappropriately bright and heavy silk saris. In short, the otherwise refined and modest Miss Puri was now the garish over dressed Mrs Luthra. Other than all the outward embellishments and transformations, I noticed an intangibility about her new self, a discomfort and restlessness, as if the old Miss Puri was still lurking underneath all the superficial glamour. One afternoon I stood next to her as she went through an essay I had written. She paused in her marking and looked up at me and smiled.

"Do you find me changed?" she asked me suddenly, lowering her voice so that the rest of the class could not hear. I hesitated, before I answered, and I knew she expected nothing but the truth from me, nevertheless that day I lied to my teacher for the first time.

"No Ma'am, you look perfect", I said, not really answering her question. She knew I was lying and I felt sad and embarrassed, as she looked away from me and continued correcting my notebook.

It was Mrs Luthra's idea that I should visit her at home for extra tuition in Hindi. There was no obvious reason for my needing extra help, except that perhaps I did not show as much passion for the subject as I did others. At that time it thrilled me to think that I would have the exclusive opportunity to gain an insight into the personal life of one of our teachers. My friends were all rather envious when I told them, and made me promise to give them all details after my visits.

At home my parents were surprised when I mentioned Mrs Luthra's offer. Like most middle class Bengali's at the time they had high academic aspirations for me, their only child. Yet, education in the city which they had reluctantly adopted as their home was getting more expensive by the day and the thought of paying for extra tuition did not make them happy. They discussed Mrs Luthra's intentions and decided that she was 'getting a bit greedy'. Embarrassingly they followed this up with a terse note to Mrs Luthra, which I awkwardly carried to her the following morning. Mrs Luthra smiled as she read the letter, her perfect oval face dimpled into an indulgent smile. She scribbled a note on another piece of paper and handed it to me to take home to my parents.

"It's not tuition", she said to me smiling, "tell your parents that sometimes it is nice to just have some company, and a little extra help at the same time". I wasn't quite sure whether she meant the company and help for herself or for me?

Needless to say my parents were thrilled that I would be getting free tuition, to save themselves the misery of a dented ego they decided that it was because I was such a bright student that my teacher had decided to help me boost my performance. This was what I was told to believe, but I knew that it was not the real purpose of these private lessons.

Mrs Luthra's house was not far from the West Delhi colony where we lived. My mother allowed me to walk there on my own in the afternoons on which we had arranged to meet. It wasn't a particularly affluent locality, more an upcoming cluster of houses, which once having had lofty aspirations had failed to meet them. There were many unfinished rooftops and balconies, which I passed, steel spikes and piles of hardened cement lay in odd corners of the streets like enormous mounds of vomit. The area was also busier than where we lived. A small bustling market selling vegetables and fruit erected itself five minutes away from Mrs Luthra's house at the same hour each afternoon. The house in which she lived was a small bungalow, the roof, like those around it unfinished, metal spokes jutting out from the sides, like decaying teeth in a giant grimace. At the front of the house was a small rectangular porch where there stood a shiny new Bajaj scooter. The room in which Mrs Luthra taught me was facing the front of the house, looking on to the porch and the scooter. I assumed it was the living room. There were two small windows, one facing the front and another looking onto an alley that ran along between this house and the next. Quite often a sharp stench of urine would waft through the open windows to interrupt our lesson. The room itself was stuffed with furniture. There was an ornate three-piece wood and satin upholstered sofa-set still covered in its original protective plastic. Against one wall stood a heavy wooden sideboard, which looked like it should have been appropriate in a palace, and next to this was an eight-seated dining table. This table was far too large for the room and it was therefore squeezed into the corner whilst the chairs like reluctant children who had been unjustly punished stood apart in various corners, looking unhappily towards their parent. Everything was new, and yet so incongruous. Why would they fill their room with so much new furniture if they did not have the space? I remember thinking to myself. Compared to this excess my parents' lives seemed so frugal and measured. I remember then feeling uncomfortable and ashamed with the knowledge of my teacher's surroundings and was reluctant to share this with my classmates the following day at school.

I soon realized that the lessons in Mrs Luthra's living room were a mere pretext for the companionship we soon established. We sat together on one of the heavy sofa's, next to the ponderous lion-legged coffee table, almost sliding off the plastic covers. She began by asking me to write short essays and stories, and we discussed my class and all my friends and the rest of the school. I soon got used to the room, which remained dark and gloomy even on the brightest of afternoons, our lessons interrupted occasionally by the distant yells and shouts of the vegetable vendors in the nearby market.

Although Mrs Luthra always welcomed me reservedly I soon came to appreciate that she looked forward to my visits as much as I did. She would come out of one of the inner rooms wearing a housecoat on top of her petticoat and blouse, which I recognized to be part of what she had worn earlier that day to school. I never met her husband, and she rarely mentioned him to me but I came across her mother-in-law who often wandered sluggishly into the room where we sat. She was a stern looking old lady and never smiled to acknowledge me when I stood up to greet her, instead I noticed how she darted strange, almost angry looks at her daughter-in-law, and then left in silence. At these times I felt Mrs Luthra needed me with her more than ever, as a friend and companion, in a world, to which even in the innocence of my childhood I knew that she did not belong.

Sometimes in the middle of our lesson, she would excuse herself and go to the kitchen. I knew when she had been there as she usually came back with a small plate of biscuits for me and a cup of tea for herself. As I became used to her lessons, I learned to coax little stories about her past out of her, about her childhood in a small town in Uttar Pradesh where she had spent long summer afternoons reading under a mango tree; the well in which she had dropped her favourite ring; her Grandparents who adored her. She told me that she had never really liked Delhi and one of her dreams had been to start a small school in the town where she had grown up.

"I even managed to save enough money for the venture", she told me with a sigh.

"Then why didn't you Ma'am?" I asked innocently.

She looked at me and smiled sadly, cupping my chin in her small soft hands she said

"Because, my dear child, one day you will realize how expensive a marriage is to a woman, especially one with my humble background". At the time I wasn't exactly sure of what she meant, did she mean the cost of the ceremony? I must have looked confused, so to clarify her comment Mrs Luthra looked pointedly around the room, at all the wrapped pieces of stodgy furniture and at the new Bajaj scooter that stood outside. I think I learnt that day what marriage and dowry really meant.

One afternoon as I sat waiting for her to return from her trip to the kitchen I decided to wander beyond the living room and find her for myself. I had always been inquisitive about the rest of the house, but now felt comfortable enough to let my curiosity get the better of me. I followed a short corridor to where I could hear the coughing and wheezing sound of what seemed like a pump. To the right of the corridor was the kitchen, a small dark space that could easily have been missed. I heard voices from within and reluctantly stopped and peered through a small open window that looked into the kitchen. Squatting on the floor was Mrs Luthra. Her housecoat was wrapped over her knees and her hair tied in a tight purposeful bun on the top of her head. Behind her stood her mother-in-law, hands on her hips observing her daughter-in-law squatting on the floor. Mrs Luthra held a small kerosene stove before her and as I stood there I watched as her entire back moved forward in order to push the pump in an effort to make the metal contraption ignite. I heard an empty swish of air and a strong smell of kerosene hit my nostrils. I had seen a stove like this one before, at my home, where in the evenings it was my father who lit it for my mother before she prepared our dinner. Now as I watched, the elderly mother-in-law began to mutter under her breath,

"Dreaded stove', she said, her voice hoarse and ugly as if it came from inside some mythical beast.

"Who should I curse really, the stove or your wretched father?" she asked Mrs Luthra.

"You should be grateful we have taken you in for such a cheap price. My son has been cheated, your father promised a car, where is the car? We just have to put up with that cheap scooter he gave us, he promised us so much, the scoundrel. He could not even get us a gas oven and his wretched daughter does not even know how to light a stove."

I shrank back, fearful of the bitterness and malice I detected in her voice. As I watched in mounting horror I saw the mother-in-law direct a kick towards her crouching daughter-in-law. Something inside me wanted to cry out and rush in and help, but I stood there like one of the living room chairs, lifeless and misplaced. As I heard the whoosh of the stove finally being pumped to life I slunk back into the living room amongst the heavy furniture, which for once felt comforting to me. After about ten minutes Mrs Luthra came in with the small plate of biscuits. I looked at her gentle face, the face which rightfully belonged to the young Miss Puri, but now cruelly hidden beneath the trappings of her marriage. I suddenly understood why I was there almost every day, why Mrs Luthra needed me to sit in that dark room with her as a sentinel to the rest of her existence and as a reminder of who she really was or had been. As she sat next to me I lifted my hand and wiped a small tear that hung desolately at the corner of her right eye. She knew then that I understood.

That was the last time I visited Mrs Luthra in her home. I looked at her expectantly in class the following day hoping that regardless of what I had discovered our lessons would continue, but she avoided me and I never got the chance to ask. Although I initially missed those afternoons and her company, I slowly got used to the idea of not going again. My parents discussed it amongst themselves and I heard them conclude that Mrs Luthra had probably done enough for me as a tutor especially since my as my grades were now consistently good. They thought no more of it and I was relieved that they never looked beyond the academic purpose of my visits.

In January of the following year as we stood for morning assembly, the cold Delhi fog swirling uncomfortably around our exposed knees, our headmistress announced that the previous evening Mrs Luthra had tragically died in a kitchen accident. Apparently the stove on which she had been cooking had burst in her face, a not uncommon incident that occurred with a chilling consistency in Delhi households at the time. I remember how the news shocked me so much that I felt faint and short of breath and had to kneel down in the dusty playground to regain my composure. Later that day as we sat in class writing out a note of condolence for her family I couldn't help but think of all the heavy furniture and the shiny Bajaj scooters and of all the Mrs Luthra's of the world squatting on the floors struggling to ignite their stoves.

The Chair

Finally they carried him down in the armchair, which had sat morosely at the head of the teak dining table. It was an old chair, tired and scratched and the red and blue silk fabric of the seat looked dull and frayed. In this nondescript third floor flat which looked upon nothing but a dry patch of featureless grassland, the chair had irrevocably given up trying to find the niche where it rightfully belonged, but then nothing seemed to fit in anymore.

The chair had been with them for the last twenty years, bought in Delhi where they had moved soon after their marriage, until six years ago when it had moved again with them to their Victorian semi in England. There it had tried to muster up the same revered position as it had in the vast apartment in their exclusive Delhi Enclave. But now all their furniture and belongings, accumulated over the years to accommodate their flamboyant lifestyles had been stuffed into this tiny flat where they had hastily moved last month when Prashant had finally given up his job and the house which came with it. Now cowering under the low yellow ceilings everything seemed incongruous and out of place. The regal settee with its stylishly jumbled array of cushions; the dining table and it's twelve tired chairs; their colonial-style four poster bed; the tasteful lamps which

Gayatri had picked out at the Cottage Industry showrooms, and which had once resided elegantly in large marble-floored hallways; the masks and pictures and trinkets which Prashant had accumulated on his far-flung travels and the various rugs and durries which were now rolled up and stood behind the doors like stern sentinels of a forgotten time. Like the chair, nothing seemed to belong here now, not even the inhabitants.

*

Gayatri had been up since dawn, cramming things into their already bulging suitcases. Prashant watched her from the bed where she had propped him up on three large pillows to hold his emaciated body. He noticed an unusual randomness to her movements. She would be carrying an armful of bottles and jars from their bathroom cupboard and then suddenly stop and stare at herself in the wardrobe mirror which had swung open to show the dusty bare shelves. Then, almost as if an imaginary key had stopped turning in her back, she would sit there for minutes on end, her brows furrowed, and her otherwise beautiful face sagging desperately downwards as if a heavy weight had been suspended from her chin. Then as suddenly as she had stopped she would jump up again with renewed energy and vigour. It was almost as if she needed to pause to recharge herself, to remind herself that what was happening was not a bizarre dream or a figment of her imagination. She barely glanced at him as she packed away her nightdress and the clothes she had worn the day before then suddenly remembered to push a pouch of silver jewellery into her hand baggage.

He stared woefully as she pulled on her jeans after her shower and let her short dark hair lie wet against her shoulders. Her movements had not lost their sensuousness even after the stresses and strains of the past few months and he wondered what she would do after he was gone. Ever so briefly he let his mind yearn for her touch, the warmth of her healthy limbs, and the softness of her dusky skin against the papery rasping of his own sickliness. The last time they had made love he had not known that between them under the heat of the sheets was another living being, a malicious thriving parasite that had quietly grown onto his insides. When she whispered in his ear, there was an echo inside him; a stirring that he had felt and thought was just his inner undying lust for her. That was sixteen months ago, before they had found out.

It all began the day he came back from his trip to Singapore carrying for her a brightly coloured dragon mask, which he had picked up from the novelty shop at the airport. Over the years he had become accustomed to bringing a token from his travels back for her. She was so house proud, so pleased to be able to put another global relic on their mantelpiece, or on the coffee table. Their home, wherever they went, resembled a small museum. When the living room could offer no more corners to stand swan etched Korean vases, Japanese Netsuke and Pakistani mosaics, they had spilled into the corridors where one entered under a Tibetan banner of peace, the floor covered in an Afghan rug whilst a golden reclining Buddha lay cold and unimpressed at the bottom of the stairs. Even the cord pull for the light in the bathroom was a bell that he had acquired from a travelling Monk at a roadside in Indonesia.

When the vomiting began they were caught unexpectedly, unaware that his body was capable of such an undignified bout of pain and unease. They had always enjoyed the rudest of health. As a couple they always seemed vibrant and energetic. When they were married, she barely nineteen and he twenty-three, the Kolkata elite had talked about them for days. It was an auspicious day, a day that offered perfection, a day that would stay stamped in the minds of all those who were there. She was a dark beauty, sullen and unsmiling throughout their wedding ceremony. Around the fire she followed him seven times, her deep almond eyes looking upon her red-rimmed *alta* painted feet. He could not take his eyes off her. His friends teased him about it later, they always would remind him, as he reminded her in moments of intimacy, how much more he loved her than she did him. In his white embroidered *Kurta* and *dhoti* he had looked young and deliciously appealing. As they stood next to each other after the ceremony their fingers touched briefly amidst the layers and ruffles of the silks they wore. They paused to look into each other's eyes as she removed the glossy, heart-shaped *paan* leaf, which she had used to cover her face as, was customary. Surrounded by cheers and applause, the crowds were oblivious to the exchanged hints of longing and desire as their eyes met. They barely found a moment to speak to each other amidst the festivities that followed the ceremony. Later on that evening, as giggling friends and cousins escorted her to the flower-bedecked bridal chamber she felt her heart leap with anticipation as she saw him waiting for her. They talked all night to make up for the silences of the day, about the future, about their hopes and aspirations and needs, now that they were finally together. As a pale pink dawn crept past the darkness of the night they reached for each other tenderly amongst the heady odours of the crushed white *rajnigandha* flowers strewn across their bed.

Five years ago, on their twenty fifth wedding anniversary, they both looked back upon their wedding day. They glanced covertly at each other as they wandered amongst their guests, in the garden of their company house on the outskirts of Egham on a glorious English summer day, and wondered how much they had changed over the years. They looked older but still quite amazingly youthful in their movements. Her face was leaner, etched with the pain of childbirth, of troubles with the in-laws, of moving with him from India to England where she had been so homesick. He looked taller, his hair a shock of dignified silver and there was a stealth in his movements which came with success. In the middle of the garden the table was spread with food and drink. Guests looked happy and content as they helped themselves to the generous spread. Gayatri had cooked the fish herself; just the way Prashant liked it, red hot and yet with a hint of sweetness. There were mounds of fried rice, of frittered aubergines and small potatoes in a tomato sauce served with the inevitable *loochis*. Gayatri took an almost empty plate of kebabs to the kitchen where she replenished it with hot ones from the oven and then garnished them with sliced raw onions. As she turned to head outside again she bumped into a smiling Prashant, a tumbler of whisky in his right hand. He blocked her way as she tried to leave the kitchen, playfully flirting with her.

"A kiss for the old husband?" he had asked her, teasing.

"Really, Prashant, how many of those have you downed?" she asked him sternly as he stood leaning against the door.

"Not enough my darling" he said and lurched forward to get closer to his wife. Gayatri had pushed him roughly back against the wall with her free hand.

"Enough of that whisky" she had spat out uncomfortably "It will be the end of you."

Prashant's smile disappeared as he let her pass, the earthy smell of her new *tashar* sari leaving him slightly giddy. He wondered where he had lost her, why they never talked like they used to, why she shunned his touch. In the garden Gayatri laid out the kebabs, smiling at her friends, yet her heart was left at the kitchen door wishing she could have been anything but cruel to him.

Later, amidst the friends whom they had collected to dissipate the growing discomfort they felt in their own company, they barely glanced at each other again. They remained a couple much admired by all around them, yet somehow the admiration they owed each other had dissolved and trickled away in a rivulet of regretful tears. Their marriage to all onlookers was that of grace and perfection, their achievements envied by all. Gayatri created the perfect home for her husband and son whilst Prashant was at the peak of his profession. Wherever they went they gathered around themselves an entourage of friends, of straggling family who they hooked up from floundering alien surrounds and pulled into their own circle. Their home, on weekends and holidays was always teeming with people, children and adults as Gayatri and Prashant sailed amongst them seeing to their needs, entertaining them with their outward sparkle and charisma whilst inwardly their greatest fear was being left alone together.

*

At first she had blamed him as she had done in all their thirty years of marriage for his constant over indulgence, for drinking too much whisky, for eating too much rich food.

"At fifty you should take better care of yourself," she almost screamed at him as he had sat despondent after throwing up for the eleventh time that day.

"I am not always going to be around to look after you, you know?"

He hated her when she was so angry, so petulant; reminding him of the role of carer that she had played for so long to him and their now dispassionate son Kaustav. There was a silent bitterness in her which he always avoided confronting, a resentment that had evolved wordlessly over the years as he became more successful as their son left home and she began to feel unwanted, aimless in her role as wife and mother. Behind the closed doors of their perfect marriage there lay a sad emptiness as she tried to find something for herself. She had been the devoted surrendered wife, and now after all these years she looked back and found that somewhere along the road to perfection she had lost herself. In her attempt to keep the house looking perfect and the cogwheels of their home working smoothly she had never attempted to do anything of her own. She looked at the young girls her son sometimes brought home with him from University and secretly she envied their nonchalant disinterest in worldly goods and domesticity. She watched as they came and went as they pleased, spent their own money on movies and eating out, dressed the way they liked. What had she been doing when she was their age? She often thought to herself. Those years after her marriage and the birth of Kaustav were just a blur. She remembered moments and faces, but none of those memories held anything special for her. She had been a mere onlooker to the life that she made for others.

Prashant felt guilty when she complained, when she nagged him to take her back to Kolkata where she could at least immerse herself in the sounds and sights and everyday clamour that she was so used to and loved. Here in the cold dampness of England, in their house that tried desperately to resemble a corner of what they knew to be home, she wept the evenings away watching old Hindi movies and gaudy game shows and television serials on Indian cable channels. At night she scribbled letters to her sisters and mother, sitting in the study till the early hours, noting down for them every detail of her monotonous life and sealing every envelope with a tear. She never posted them.

He travelled more in an attempt to forget the gilded cage in which he had kept his precious bird of paradise. Those were the days before they found out how far the poison had already spread within him, how rampant that cancerous growth had become in his body. Those were distant days now, he wished he hadn't over indulged, wished he hadn't drunk too much, wished he had listened to her whilst his body was still healthy and he could do something about it. Just wished!

*

She sat next to him in the cold polished corridor of Hammersmith hospital. She always accompanied him even though sometimes he had begun to wish she didn't. She let him drive to the hospital and sat beside him in the passenger seat and guided him through the unfamiliar roads of London and then back to Egham in the evening. Every week for six months they did this as a routine on Tuesdays. He would wake up from his increasingly fitful nights to smell her cooking noodles or fried rice downstairs which she would then carefully pack in containers to save them having to eat the bland hospital food. It was almost as though they were going on a morbid picnic, where they sat in the hospital canteen barely speaking to each other as she picked at the cold remains of her cooking on his plate. At these times there emerged a relentless optimism in her, which annoyed him.

"This is a negative country Prashant," she had said when the Doctor had told him that he had just six months to live. "Don't believe what he says. You will be fine if we just went back to Kolkata. Do you remember how that Doctor in Howrah miraculously cured our friend Jayanti's husband? We can go to him couldn't we? To hell with what they say here."

He had listened quietly as she spoke; a fear crept over his already numb heart. Was she saying this just to go back? Did she really care about him? A cold doubt crept into his mind that mingled with the confused echoes of a man who has just been told that he will die, very soon and very painfully.

They kept up with the chemotherapy and the trial drug, which she offered him religiously first thing in the morning after which she whisked him over to the bathroom scales and weighed his withering body. He had become her project; she had found something after all these years, which she threw herself haphazardly into, without thinking of reality. She stopped writing her letters home instead she browsed for hours on the Internet, always hoping to find a site which would offer a miraculous cure. She often made long distance phone calls to a Guru who lived in an ashram at the foot of the Himalayas. Although she never spoke to him she managed to speak to his disciples and always came off the phone with renewed energy and vigour whilst Prashant cowered under her relentless optimism.

"Oh Lord why me?" he often wondered silently as he was prodded poked, opened up and then closed again by alternatively optimistic and then pessimistic surgeons and medics. The endless walks down hospital corridors, the unpacking of the noodles, the constant hopefulness of his wife, all contributed to the fears, which Prashant faced when alone in his bed at night. He cringed at the thought of the pity and false flirtatiousness of the nurses who he met, the sadness in their eyes when Gayatri showed them photographs of him taken just a few months before it all changed.

He was scared now, every time she blew her endless optimism in his face. Talk of going to health camps in India run by popular spiritual leaders who vowed to cure every ailment with a handful of herbs and a few breathing techniques, her constant obsession with calling the family astrologer and the Guru in the Himalayan foothills, every time he showed any other symptom of the relentless disease which his body was battling against. One room in their house was devoted to the Gods who she was convinced would show mercy on them and miracles could happen. Every day after her morning shower she would stand before the long array of idols which she had brought with her, eyes closed, hands together, her sensuous mouth mumbling desperately to the unseen presence. One day the curtains caught fire from her incense stick left after her prayers too close to the fabric. After the fire brigade had left she and Prashant stood at the door of the now smouldering room where the stench of burnt fabric made him want to retch.

"It's a sign," Gayatri said, "Someone is listening to me up there and wants to do something for us."

She put her palms together and started praying again to the now rather dishevelled-looking images and idols on the blackened windowsill. Prashant had stood quietly besides her reeling under the weight of her hopes for his recovery, for her plans for the future.

Three months later, after many stays in the hospital, after numerous visits from friends and well-wishers he was left completely and utterly at her mercy. When friends visited them, Gayatri and Prashant were now often barely aware of their presence, so preoccupied were they in the roles of patient and carer. Oblivious to their presence she sometimes walked him back and forth from the toilet when he needed it and later even went in with him and held him on the seat. Outside the door their friends watched them, uncomfortable at this intimacy and the crossing of boundaries, which were never really meant to be crossed. His once handsome face was now twisted with pain, his body a monstrous bundle of bones and skin. As he lost weight her desperation grew and Prashant, in the seemingly fewer lucid moments which he now had, wished she would just sit quietly next to him, hold his hand instead of fussing. He turned his face away from her like a petulant child as she brought him mashed bananas, opened pots of baby food in the hope that he would eat and recover. She scolded him when he would not do the yoga exercises which were guaranteed to cure him, but as his body grew frailer it hurt even to bend and she soon gave up.

One day just after they had moved to their new flat, she led him to the window which looked upon the stretch of grass where a few children played with a bright ball and some teenagers stood around the fringe. It was a warm evening, unusual for the time of year and Gayatri stood next to him as he leant against her shoulder. She felt how cold his skin had become how his hands shook like an old man's as he steadied himself by holding the ledge.

"Can you see the children playing?" She asked him softly, her breath warm upon his shoulder. She looked into his face, the grey stubble upon his sallow skin, the parched lips.

"Like Kaustav played," he whispered. "Remember in the park in Delhi." his voice trailed off, the last words a mere rasp.

"Yes, and he would refuse to come in to do his homework, until you got home from work." said Gayatri smiling at the memory.

"Yes," he croaked, "I remember. He was such hard work, so much mischief in him." He paused, and then added, almost as an afterthought, "You were so beautiful then."

She thought she had misheard him, or perhaps he was rambling as he sometimes did when he had a morphine shot. She looked away from him hastily, uncomfortable suddenly not wanting him to say anymore.

"Will you remarry when I am gone?" He whispered now and turned to look at her, his neck aching with each movement costing him ounces of his meagre stores of energy. He could see her ears flush red in an instant as he remembered they used to when she was awkward or embarrassed.

"What are you saying? Nothing is going to happen to you," she insisted, but her voice quavered momentarily and she moved her head further away so that he could not see her face.

"Gayatri, Gayatri," he said gently, and shook his poor dying shoulders. "You must remarry. Somebody like Samaresh or Nikhil. Either of them will be a good husband."

"Don't, please don't," she pleaded.

When she turned towards him he could see the tears rolling down her cheeks along with the remnants of her dark eyeliner. He did not say anymore but took her warm hand in his own and they wept silent tears together as they watched the children play outside in the growing twilight. Just as they had watched their son play so many years ago.

Through her tears she gratefully smiled for his silence and then took his elbow and led him back to the bedroom where he sank onto the pillows, his weeping bedsores drilling holes in his aching body.

They never spoke again about the future. There were always too many people around and his moments awake and lucid became fewer as the days went by. The constant flow of visitors, friends and families, Doctors and health workers helped to keep their silences and their tears at bay. At night she looked after him like a patient, waking with him, turning him, and giving him his medicine and sips of water.

Sometimes he noticed impatience in her, a tired irritability as her body suffered under the strains of the uncertainty of her situation. He winced as she dressed him, pulled up his socks roughly onto his sore swollen oozing feet, and almost forced the food into his clenched lips. He was scared of her obsessions, her need to feel that he would survive, knowing in her heart that he did not have much time. When the Doctors finally gave up on him, withdrew the offers of help, they knew the decision was made for them. They had to take him back home.

*

So today was the day they were flying back to Kolkata. In her own mind, Gayatri had been debating for months now whether they should make this last move. Every couple of months over the past year she had made new plans and changed the old, with every kilo of weight he lost and every round of the chemotherapy, she had rearranged the present as the future looked more depressing. Now there was nothing left for them here except a handful of aching memories.

Friends and family poured into the flat from the early hours. There was a forced cheer in the flat that morning. Everyone relieved to see the other, awkwardness about how to say goodbye momentarily forgotten in the mock jollity and concerns of the task ahead. Cases were counted and heaved down the stairs, tickets were checked and re-checked, Windows closed, cupboards emptied, keys handed over for safekeeping. A hundred little chores masked the real concerns in everyone's mind. How could they say goodbye?

The question remained as to how they would get him onto that chair. They debated amongst themselves, there was a great plumping of pillows, and the chair was moved at different angles, sometimes facing him, sometimes away from him. There was a gentle argument as to how he should be lifted. One young man, the son of Prashant's old colleague from Delhi, picked up the chair and demonstrated for the rest of them how it should be angled, so that its fragile load would not slide off. Prashant looked on from his place on the bed, his bedsores wept for him, now painlessly as the morphine which he had begged for an hour ago had numbed his body. His shoulders ached though from the weight of his neck, each hair felt heavy, his eyes like stones rolling in empty hard sockets. The corners of his mouth felt dry but each time he rasped for water no one heard him, they were too busy organising how they would take him to the airport.

When two of Kaustav's friends bent over him as the willing volunteers who would lift him out of the bed onto the chair, he shrunk back in fear. Their strong healthy hands hurt as they touched his sore, thin skin. The tears fell soundlessly from his eyes as he whispered her name.

"Gayatri," he said over and over again.

They smiled at him, good young men with clear honest hearts, here to help their friend's family, the man whose home they had spent many a jolly evening in over the last six years, whose house had become an oasis for their lives in this friendless place. Their concern was that although Prashant was now so light, a mere nineteen kilograms, he was awkward to carry, and he would need something to grip especially when they would manoeuvre him down the curved staircase from their apartment on the third floor.

They leaned over him, sweet morning tea breath, and their eyes bright with eagerness. He winced and they struggled to hold him up, his arms shook as they tried to grip him gently from underneath, they were nervous, not wanting to hurt him now.

Then Gayatri walked in. She had sent down the luggage to the cavalcade of cars waiting downstairs, she was checking the locks on the windows making sure the appliances were all turned off. He looked at her beseechingly, his sunken eyes shining from the heap in which he lay on the bed. She looked at him across the room, over the heads of the eager helpers, through the haze of good wishes that surrounded him.

They moved aside when she walked through to him, and bent over him gently, the gratitude in his eyes made them avert their own. They could not look as she bent down and lifted him tenderly like she would have done to their child; his arm went over her shoulder and his silvery white head rested momentarily on her bosom. They moved the chair forward so that she could seat him on it promptly, and she placed him on it and then slowly she arranged his arms his legs his waist, his swollen blood- speckled feet, until she knew he was as comfortable as a dying man could be. His hand lingered over her head for a few moments, as if he was blessing her, she looked at him, their eyes met and something unspoken passed between them. In that moment they both knew that this was their farewell. As strong arms lifted the chair, they smiled at each other knowingly as if they shared one last secret that would forever stay unlocked and then he was on his way down.

Fair and Lovely

"*Fair and Lovely Cream*" the letters on the paper packet which held the puffed rice read. "*More Than Just Fairness, Clear Fairness*".

Kamini looked at the picture of the model advertising the cream. There were two pictures, one before and one after the treatment of the fair and lovely cream. The face was that of a pretty girl, the kind of face that did not quite make it to the big screen but smiled out of endless magazines and newspapers until she became familiar to the public. The second photograph partially lost in the folds of the bottom of the paper bag showed the same face but perceptibly fairer than the first one. Her smile was now wider, happier than when her skin had been a couple of shades darker.

Kamini lifted the packet, careful not to spill the puffed rice, and looked at the picture as she walked home, trying not to notice her own dark hands which held it. It would be a miracle, she thought ruefully, if like the girl on the packet she could turn a few shades fairer than what she currently was. Perhaps then, she could have refused the advances of Harinath Bhowmik. If only she were fairer she could have chosen to marry whom she wanted and not wait for him to choose her. Perhaps? If things were fairer.

It was a clammy summer evening in the village where Kamini lived with her mother. Her bare feet kicked up the red dust familiar to Bengal, as she walked back home along the huddles of awkward houses that made up the village of Bauria. She passed by the pond where women were now taking their evening dip, the green waters sparkling, their chatter mingled with the gentle laps of the water against their bodies. They seemed to have an entire afternoon's gossip to exchange.

A group of children in ragged clothes ran past Kamini, rolling an old rubber tyre with a stick, whilst a naked and snotty-nosed infant wailed behind them, trying to keep up. The houses grew smaller as she reached the edge of the village, more crooked and desperate. Beyond were the stretches of paddy fields, which were now dry, waiting for the rains to come and rescue the crop. It had been a long hot summer; the sun had baked the small village to a crust and each day Kamini had awoken to fiery skies wishing she could go back to the artificial comforts of Delhi where she had been for the last fifteen years. But it had been her own decision to come back to the village where she was born, to be with her mother, now broken and alone after Kamini's father's death.

It had been a struggle to leave the city. Mashima, her employer, had been so reluctant, had tried so hard to persuade her to stay, and had relied upon Kamini's loyalties to the family whom she had worked for so many years. After fifteen years in which she had only gone back to the village once for her father's funeral, Kamini knew that now it was time to close the chapter of her life in Delhi.

Fifteen years ago she had made the two-day train journey across the plains alone. She was twelve years old then, thin and lanky, her hair infested with lice. Mashima, the rather stern and loud-voiced lady of the house, had immediately sorted this out by making her rub pungent kerosene oil into her hair. After this she was made to keep her hair in a short bob. She remembered how she had cried as the barber had chopped off her waist-long tresses, under the strict supervision of Mashima. She had been given new bedding, an acrid-smelling bar of Lifebuoy soap and a blue and yellow polka dot *salwar kameez*. This last item she was particularly in awe of; in the village where she grew up she had owned nothing but a couple of tattered muddy dresses, from which she would graduate to wearing saris. The *salwar kameez* was a sign of the modern world to Kamini and she had looked at it fearfully when Mashima had handed it to her.

Her bed on the floor of the children's room was more than she had experienced back home. Cool air conditioning in the hot summer months and warm cotton filled *razai* in the winter. She learnt to cook on a gas burner, chop vegetables with a knife instead of a *boati,* the floor-based knife blade used in the villages of Bengal, and she became adept at loading and sorting whites and colours into the washing machine. She woke early in the morning and made sandwiches for the children's lunch boxes, then made sure she had set out their clean, pressed uniforms. She watched as their mother persuaded them to have their bananas and almonds, buttered toast and bowls of freshly made yoghurt. Kamini herself sat down to her breakfast after they had left for school, strong tea and rotis. Sometimes she would have half a leftover banana before her own breakfast. Mashima was kind to Kamini, yet authoritative in her running of the house. Soon after she had arrived in Delhi, Mashima heard Kamini whimpering in her sleep at night. The following morning she asked her in a perfunctory way if she would like to go back to the village to her parents.

"It can be arranged you know, if necessary. I do not wish you to be unhappy in your service here," she had said firmly, her eyes bearing down on Kamini as she sat on the kitchen floor peeling potatoes for lunch.

But Kamini had looked down upon the potatoes and shook her head. She knew that the money she sent to her parents meant a lot to them. Her father had rarely held a job for long in the various roles as farm labourer. As he got older and slower he mostly stayed at home. Notoriously lazy, he spent the days feeding off his wife's meagre income, which she earned from selling fish at the local rail-side market. Kamini could not go back, at least not yet, besides she was beginning to get used to the comforts of city living, the wholesome three course meals which she sat eating on the kitchen floor, the gaudy television serials she watched whilst massaging Mashima's feet in the quiet of the afternoons. There had been too much to hold her back there then, so much that she soon found she was unwilling to give up.

Her mother was in the cow shed when Kamini returned with the packet of puffed rice. She could hear her singing to their cow called Nandini; a bony creature, with an eye impediment. The cow's eyes watered dark rivulets against her white face, as if she was constantly weeping. Ever since her father had died Kamini's mother seemed to spend more and more of her time in the cowshed. The half-starved cow she had bought with her meagre savings seemed to be the centre of the retired fisher woman's existence.

Early in the morning she would feed the beast, clean its milky grey coat with water mixed with its own milk. Then she would carefully coax it to give more milk, its udders shuddering as she sat beneath them, silky strands of milk jetting out into the pail with a steely clang that rung eerily through the shed. Once Kamini had tried her hand at it, the pulsating skin of the udders in her hand had made her uneasy, and she was terrified of being kicked in the face by the animal. Back in Delhi she was used to going out to the 'mother dairy' milk booth in the evenings, swinging her pail of milk, bantering with the friendly Sikh gentleman who ran the place. There, the milk frothed out of the twinjets above her pail, a huge electronic sterilised udder. It was on one such trip that she had met Umesh the manservant from the house across the road. At first they had reluctantly acknowledged each other, whether at the milk booth or in the market buying fish. Sometimes Kamini caught sight of him washing the owner's car as she stood on the roof putting out the washing.

The families they worked for were friendly enough not to make a fuss over the slowly noticeable friendship between them. At first it was just a few words at the milk booth, a wave from the balcony and a friendly exchange at the market. Later, on Kamini's eighteenth birthday they had met secretly for the first time at the local movie theatre. Soon this became a habit. It was easy to slip away for a few hours in the afternoon when the mistress was asleep. Later they would kiss furtively in the dark, hands fumbling with their clothes, skin against illicit skin. At night Kamini stayed awake thinking of Umesh. She thought of how they could make a future together in Delhi. She dreamt of having a family of her own, about sending her children to good schools in the city. She fantasised about living in the servants quarters of one of the elite mansions she had seen in the adjoining neighbourhood. Her ambitions had their limitations, seamless boundaries that involved a few comforts and happiness.

Kamini and Umesh continued to meet in secret for three years. They grew closer and Kamini even began to hint to her parents in her letters home about the young man she was hoping to marry soon. Those were the best three years for Kamini in the city. She was now a pleasant-looking young woman, dark and thin, hair still cut in a severe bob which tucked behind her ears looked quite fetching at times. She learnt to take care of the way she looked and dressed. Secretly she used the oils and unguents which were displayed on Mashima's dressing table, hoping she could partake of some of the healthy glamour of the older woman.

One hot summer evening, whilst watering the wilting plants in rooftop pots, she heard a commotion from the house across the street. This was the house where Umesh worked. Peering over the low wall on the roof she saw a figure in a red sari standing by their door, her shrill voice carried up to where Kamini stood, her arms gesticulating agitatedly. Beside her, almost hidden in the depths of his mother's sari, stood a little boy, perhaps four or five years old. Kamini did not quite catch what the woman in the red sari was saying, a few words floated over to her filtered through the hiss and hum of the coolers and air conditioners from all the neighbouring houses.

"Husband," and "Village," was all she heard repeatedly.

Later, downstairs as she deftly made the rotis for dinner her mistress came and stood quietly next to her in the kitchen.

"Did you know what happened at the Chatterjee's this afternoon?" she asked fiddling awkwardly with the cutlery as she spoke.

"No Mashima, Ki? What happened? I heard some noises" Kamini said innocently curious.

"It's Umesh," said Mashima, her voice awkward, desperate to get this over and done with. She had known about Kamini's feelings for Umesh for a while now, and though she never openly encouraged the relationship, secretly she felt it was a good match for the girl. She was uncomfortable about discussing it with her.

"He seems to have had a wife and child in the village all this time," she said, her voice low and embarrassed.

"Apparently he has been promising to go back to his family for a while. Today his wife, fed up with his promises came to fetch him herself," she concluded. She looked at Kamini, at the back of her slender neck, the small scar where she had been recently cut by the barber's razor. There was a stillness about her shoulders which was perturbing, Mashima was unsure of what to say next. It was after all not her position to discuss the servant's love affairs, yet she was fond of the girl, knowing how hard she worked and how lonely it could be growing up in the big city.

"Chalo, men are like that in every station of life," she said being worldly-wise "Never trust them."

She tried to sound cheerful after this phrase, but her nervous smile revealed the untruth in her words. Momentarily she almost reached out to touch Kamini's hunched shoulders, to comfort her, but she hesitated, caught between her own emotions and status as her superior. She left the kitchen to see to the children and her husband waiting for their dinners in front of the television. Kamini had continued to make the rotis. They tasted hard and bitter that evening mixed with her tears and unhappiness. For once no one complained and life went on as usual.

*

"Ma, I have the *moori* here," said Kamini, peering into the darkness of the shed, the shadows from the setting sun filtering into the small space. Kamini could barely discern the outline of the wizened figure of her mother sitting on a stool and making dung cakes. She heard the mass squelching between her fingers as she kneaded it together ready to be slapped against the side of their wall embellished with her finger marks. After they had dried in the caking sun over the next few days Kamini would come and peel them off ready to be used for fuel in their little cooking oven. The cow mooed noisily in the corner, a hollow echo that rattled the insides of the house.

"Come Ma have some milk and moori," she said as she lifted up the half-empty pail of milk waiting near the doorstep. Her mother followed her indoors in a little while, wiping her hands on the already filthy edges of her sari. Momentarily, Kamini thought of the endless array of saris and jewellery which Mashima used to wear. Each day she wore a fresh one in the evening and one in the morning. In summers it would be lovely starched cotton in pale blues and mauves and peach; in the Delhi winters it would be brightly coloured silks which shimmered elegantly in the winter sunshine. Here her mother had two saris, exactly the same, and each with a thin dark border, the traditional attire of a Bengali widow. Each day she immersed herself fully-clothed into the local pond and washed the one she was wearing. Then she deftly changed into the dry one. Neither of them looked clean.

Kamini's own wardrobe had been the cause of many looks from the rest of the villagers when she had come back home. Her *salwar* suits in various styles and colours were seen as incredibly fashionable. At first she had felt proud to show them off to the gaping villagers. She had felt so different from them, so aloof. Over the years nothing had changed back here, in this tired shanty of a village, whereas she herself no longer remembered the Kamini who had once lived here. It wasn't just her hair, or her clothes, or the fact that she painted her nails or wore shoes. It was something more than that, inside her, the experiences that had changed her forever. Slowly her need to show off her wardrobe wore off. Now all she wished was to wear something clean, washed in soap and clear water not in the putrid depths of the pond where the entire village bathed. When her second pair of sandals snapped she decided to walk barefoot like most of the villagers.

As she poured the puffed rice into a bowl for her mother she looked at her sitting on her haunches, her eyes glazed and weary. Kamini knew that her mother's mind wandered a lot nowadays, that she never seemed to be herself. This was also the reason why Kamini had reluctantly agreed to get married, to meet the prospective grooms who her mother had encouraged. Although her mother eagerly told the grooms and their families how accomplished her daughter was and how well she had done in all her years in the city, they usually left shaking their heads, put off by the darkness of her skin, even though many of the prospective grooms were rather dark themselves. After entertaining almost twenty prospective families there came Harinath.

She thought of Harinath now as she watched her mother. It was a very convenient match. He lived on the other side of the village so when they were married she could come and check on her mother whenever she needed to. That was perhaps the most attractive part of his proposition. He worked in a local jute mill, earned well and seemed quiet and reserved. When Kamini had reluctantly come out to meet Harinath and his family sitting in the small outer room of their hut, she had only looked down at his dark gnarled feet.

She heard the now-familiar click of the tongues of the women of his family as they disapproved of the colour of her skin. They bargained with her mother, asked for jewels and money if they accepted the offer, saying that no one else would marry this poor creature and how they were in actual fact doing them a favour. Kamini looked down at her own dry feet, the soles cracked from walking bare foot the sandals and chappals of Delhi wrapped in their plastic in a suitcase which she rarely looked into now.

The date had been fixed; the offer of ten saris and a thousand rupees was accepted begrudgingly. Sweets were passed around in silence. Slowly Kamini had looked up, her eyes had met Harinaths's briefly, terror gripped her throat and stomach, and she almost choked on the morsel, which the woman sitting next to her had offered her. Later on she had wept angry tears that burnt her skin as she sat outside, the night air still and dead except for the distant noise of a train screaming through the country.

Her mother slurped the last of the milk from the enamel bowl. She was happy that her daughter would be married soon. Mother and daughter waited quietly for the days to pass, they had invited the few villagers who lived close by, and had bought a yellow Banarasi sari at the local market. Now all they needed to do was wait for the day of the wedding.

Kamini thought of Umesh, his warm round face, his sharp moustache and bright eyes. It all seemed such a long time ago. Mashima had sent her a money order for five thousand rupees which she had gratefully received, her mother was proud of this, delighted that they now had some money to spare.

As the sun set behind the paddy fields Kamini knew that she had no other choice but to be here. This was where she had been born and this was where she would die. She somehow wished she had not tasted the lights and the colours of the big city, wished she had been left to sing to the cows and bathe in the ponds for all those years in between. She wished there was no such thing as coolers or air conditioners, or eyeliners and dupattas. She wished that she had not tasted chocolate and Coco Cola and the rush of a car ride through the buzz of a throbbing city, and the sweet taste of abandon, but amongst all these other things, most of all she wished that Harinath Bhowmik was not seventy years old.

The Retirement

Although Mr Mukherjee had rarely done so before, that day he ordered a taxi to carry his belongings back from the office. He had worked in the same Council Department in Kingston upon Thames for the last twenty years and now at the age of fifty-five he was retiring. That day when he shuffled out of the office building which he had walked up to each working day, and teetered over to the taxi waiting for him at the curb, the enormity of his decision lay heavily upon his shoulders.

The road glistened in the rain, a cold wind blowing icily against his neck as late afternoon shoppers ran to get home before the onset of rush hour. Upstairs on the fifth floor, his colleagues, or now ex-colleagues, were clearing up the glasses from around his cubicle where they had rather unremarkably toasted his retirement.

They had no idea why Hiren Mukherjee had decided to retire so early; it puzzled them as to why he would forego a steady income with added benefits. Most of his colleagues suspected that he had no other plans but to stay home, and they were right. He had tried to explain to them, in his gentle, subdued manner that he was needed at home, that he was happy with his decision, but somehow they had remained unconvinced. To his boss he had tried to explain himself better.

"It's my son," he muttered, disorientated by the intensity of her gaze. Looking down on the dusty toes of his brown Hush Puppies he added, sounding apologetic, "I think he needs me at home, he is at a funny age."

She had looked uncomprehendingly at Mr Mukherjee. She had never really valued him since she had been promoted to his department a couple of years ago. His work was good, but not outstanding and he rarely seemed to make an effort to be part of the team. He sat there, day after day, slumped quietly in his cubicle, smiling forlornly at her from behind his thick glasses whenever she approached with a query. As he stood in front of her now, his narrow shoulders hunched over his small potbelly, clamouring to free itself from the confines of his shirt, she felt sorry for him. Yet, she signed his resignation papers without much hesitation. He would not really be missed, she thought, but nevertheless a shame to see him go.

"Enjoy the garden," she had said to him with the cheery abandon of the young and unencumbered, as he left her office. It took him a moment to comprehend her allusion to the garden. Their small plot adjoining the house was almost non-existent. He and Anjali had never been keen gardeners, nor had they ever felt the need to be outside on warm summer days. Over the years it had become unsightly and overgrown, frowned upon by their next-door neighbours. It was more like a storage area than anything else, with a few upturned wrought iron chairs and a rotten teak table. He smiled vaguely back at his boss, but her young blonde head had already turned away from him, and she was staring at her computer screen.

Mr Mukherjee filled the cardboard box with his stapler, his pens and an assortment of papers and magazines, which he had collected over the years. There were a few books tucked away in a bottom drawer, which he had almost forgotten about. He picked one up and dusted the cover. It was a pale blue book of Hindu baby names. He stood leafing through the pages, looking at the names, which he had underlined almost fifteen years ago when they were expecting their child.

Abhigaan, Bashishta, Dhananjaya,

Long, complicated names, which he had loved, but knew grudgingly, would not be practical. They had decided upon *Sandip,* simple and easily pronounced. He came to the page with names starting with S. There was a question mark next to Sandip. He smiled as he saw this, the question mark still followed him, he thought philosophically.

Pulling himself away from the book of names he saw a guide to teenage years staring up at him from the drawer, the cover sporting the confident face of a Doctor who was also the proud father of five teenage boys. Mr Mukherjee recalled how he had barely been able to understand the Doctor's approach to taming teenagers. The book had suggested having lengthy discussions, time out on holiday, encouraging teenagers to do as they pleased. All this Mr Mukherjee had found unfamiliar. He remembered not even being able to get past the first few pages; he wondered whose lives these books were based on? Where did these seemingly perfect families live?

There were no photographs on his desk. Most of his co-workers had framed pictures of their families, their friends, moments on holiday, adoring dogs and cats, and even themselves as people who had lives apart from their office, lounging around on beaches, smiling cheek-to-cheek with girlfriends and boyfriends.

Mr Mukherjee just had a small red and yellow picture of the Goddess Durga pinned to his notice board above his desk. The picture, once a page from a Bengali calendar, had faded over the years and the resplendent ten-armed Goddess looked distant and unconcerned. Now there were holes on the Goddess's magnificent gold headdress, where he had pinned it time and again, moving it around to different points on the board.

All this he carefully loaded into his box and took down to the taxi, which the security guard downstairs, had called. Mr Mukherjee wondered momentarily whether this would require a tip. He was not very comfortable with money; awkwardness overcame him, the thought of the tip being refused being more embarrassing than its acceptance. In the end, he decided against it; his hands were too full with his box to enable him to reach into his pockets.

As the taxi pulled away, he looked up at the building, the well-lit fifth floor and the shadows of all those people whom he had known for so long and yet barely known at all; the cubicle where he had sought refuge on those days where being at home was unbearable, the small canteen where he had often enjoyed a cup of tea in silence. Yet now he was giving up that miniscule haven of peace to stay at home for good.

He shivered slightly at the thought. The decision had been his own though, he had no one to blame for his actions. As they turned a corner, the lights of the office melted into the evening, and the dark insides of the taxi enveloped the solitude of Mr Mukherjee's decision.

He paid the taxi driver outside his home in New Malden. The only other time he remembered coming home in a taxi was when Anjali had called him, distraught and hysterical, that afternoon now almost a year ago. He barely remembered the journey home that day, only recalled hearing Anjali's screams down the phone and feeling his own heart pumping fast in his rather unfit body as he had run down the office stairs. He had been terrified, not quite knowing what to expect on his return, hoping that Anjali, being Anjali, was over-reacting.

He remembered now, going back, hearing Anjali's sobs through the open front door of their small terraced house, Sandip screaming at his mother, the neighbours looking through parted curtains. He had not seen what she had seen, but he could only guess, based on Anjali's description of what she had stumbled upon when she had come home unexpectedly.

He shuddered when the recesses of his mind took him to places he did not want to go; his son, a girl, the bed, the sickly sweet smell of weed, a compromising situation which his wife had walked in upon that afternoon in February. What followed were days of venomous silence between mother and son, only broken by the awkwardness of his own voice mediating between the two, trying desperately to understand why things were happening the way they were. It was then that he had decided that a change was inevitable; he needed to do something to alter the festering situation at home. It was time to do things his own way.

Before Hiren Mukherjee had married Anjali, he had been a confirmed bachelor. Somehow, in his late thirties he found it more and more difficult to imagine himself living with another person. He was used to his own quiet ways, the simplicity of his everyday existence. He was never bored or lonely, but pressure from his aging parents began to weigh him down, until he found himself seriously considering the prospects of getting married. In Kolkata - where his parents now lived, his father retired from his position as a Headmaster - he had been to see many prospective brides, but somehow, until he saw Anjali, he had never felt the inclination to let someone into his life.

He was surprised to learn how eligible he was in Kolkata. He was an average looking fellow, a qualified cost accountant, with a steady job in a small Council Department in England. He did not smoke or drink excessively and there had never been any scandals attached to his name. His parents and relatives vouched for the integrity of Hiren Mukherjee every time he was introduced to a new round of prospective in laws.

"Our boy, has never glanced in the direction of a woman," an elderly Uncle had once announced confidently in front of a room full of strangers. Hiren had squirmed quietly in the corner. How did his Uncle know this for a fact?

He had thought briefly of the time he had spent one afternoon, peering through his bedroom window at his young blonde next-door neighbour, sunbathing in her garden. In his mind he had touched her bare skin, the silky smoothness of her shoulders, fantasised about her for days after. He knew he was no saint. Once at College he had fumbled with the top buttons of a fellow student. She had been drunk and willing and thrown herself upon him as a dare with her own group of friends. Finally, Hiren had abandoned his attempts, overwhelmed by the reek of alcohol on her breath and the filthy whispers in his ear. But perhaps, no one need ever know this, he thought uncomfortably.

One summer whilst visiting his elderly Aunt he had met Anjali for the first time. In the famous *Bancharam* sweet shop, queuing up for an evening round of sweet *jibe gaja,* Hiren had eyed Anjali's long glossy plait of hair and afterwards, his hands dripping with warm brown packets of *mishti* and *shingara,* he had followed her until she turned onto the landing on the second floor of the same building where his Aunt lived. After that it was easy, all Hiren needed to do was mention his interest to his Aunt. Six months later, he was boarding a flight from Kolkata airport with his new bride by his side.

At first he had been awkward sharing his small life with Anjali. In Kolkata things had been taken out of his hands and there had been few opportunities to meet her let alone get to know her, until he found her crying quietly next to him on the flight. He was unsure of how to comfort her, and had finally handed her a rather grubby white handkerchief which she had refused. They flew to London in near silence.

He had shown Anjali around London in the first days of their marriage in an attempt to inspire in her some enthusiasm for the novelty of her new life. He had tried to make her smile as he photographed her standing next to an impassive Queen's guard outside Buckingham Palace, but she stood there, almost as aloof as the guard himself, her long plait snaking down her left shoulder, her hands straight by her sides. And later, much to his disappointment, she had sat downstairs during the open-top bus tour, which they took, insisting that she felt cold on the top deck.

In the evenings he had come home to her cooking, which although it made a change from his own bachelor fare, he found inferior to his own culinary skills. He kept this a guilty secret for fear of offending her; unsure of whether he should offer to help as she fumbled her way around the unfamiliarity of his kitchen.

Whilst most newly wed couples thrown together in alien surrounds found comfort in each other's company, Anjali never quite shed her awkwardness. Even in their most intimate moments, which were inevitable as a married couple, there remained a distance which Hiren could never fathom.

And yet she had been far more ambitious than he had expected. A brilliant student at Kolkata University, Anjali had insisted that she be allowed to continue her research in England. It took her a few years to get into the academic system, but once this happened, Hiren quietly took a back seat as he watched his wife's career flourish. He was glad to let her go. He thought perhaps this would be the answer to her enduring detachment from him. Whilst he felt proud of her achievements there was a part of him that sometimes felt worn and tired; had he just been a means to her professional aspirations?

Over the years he never surmounted her aloofness and soon it became a hazy sense of angst, like an indistinct outline in an aging album of memories. That was why when Sandip was born as a surprise, there followed a few years of welcome change in their household. Their house was childproofed for their son, windows fixed so there would be no drafts, people put off so that their child would not be disturbed whilst he slept. Slowly, the few friends they had made over the years silently drifted away, like leaves on a forlorn path, buffeted around and then whisked into the past.

Anjali went back to work after a year at home. She never quite took to being a stay-at-home mother, but they found a good child-minder and her hours at the University were flexible enough for the guilt to be dispersed between them.

Every year, Hiren and Anjali went to Kolkata with their son in tow to meet the grandparents. For Hiren this was the most carefree time of the year; with Anjali happily involved in the depths of her own family, he was free to savour the delights of the city with Sandip. They visited the local fish markets where Sandip sat on his father's shoulders and ogled at the rows of glistening silver; unflustered by the sharp smell of the river mixed with the putrid odour of the drains. They took *Tonga* rides outside the Victoria Memorial, the slow whimsy of the horses weaving through the Kolkata traffic. He played football with a crowd of children in the green stretch of the *maidaan* as Sandip looked on in delight.

One weekend, they swam in the tranquil green waters of a *pukur* near his Grandparent's ancestral home in Howrah, and in the depths of a hot afternoon he read Sandip stories from his own favourite childhood books. Aunts, Uncles and Grandparents all doted on the little boy; they delighted in his British accent and his '*sahib*' ways, and at these times Hiren Mukherjee felt consumed with love for his son, for the innocence of his ways, his gleeful embrace of life in Kolkata.

When Sandip turned eleven, Hiren and Anjali decided that he should, as was customary, have the sacred thread ceremony. They planned their visit to Kolkata in the heat of the summer, where on an auspicious day, amongst the dust and power cuts they dragged their son to the ancient *Kali Bari*, where, patronised by red-mouthed surly priests, he sat for hours in front of a fire, bare-bodied and uncomprehending.

They shaved his head and put the thread around him; the sacred mantra whispered in his ear, his initiation into the life as a Brahmin. Hiren and Anjali had sat next to him, watching, sweltering in the heat, the clamour of the temple stifling their thoughts. They glanced at each other briefly as the priest asked them to offer their blessings. As the sacred Ganges water washed their son's newly shaved scalp, they threw the bleeding red hibiscus flowers into the offering bowl. Briefly they united in their hopes for their son, the one that tied their past and future together.

Over the next couple of years, Sandip stopped wearing the sacred thread. He felt awkward when he undressed in front of his friends in sports locker rooms. He tried to explain the significance to them, but amongst the taunting and teasing he soon realised that it would be much easier if he left it at home. Mr Mukherjee found it hanging from the corner of a picture of Michael Jackson in his room. Aghast, he had tried to explain to the thirteen year-old the importance of the thread, but Sandip remained dispassionate.

"It's part of your heritage, your culture," Hiren had explained as he looked at his son sprawled across his bed, the room in semi-darkness from the black paper Sandip had plastered over the single window. He could only vaguely see the outline of his son's face as he fiddled apathetically with his CD player. He could see the resemblance to Anjali, the firm chin, the sharp nose, the distance in his dark eyes.

"I feel like a hypocrite if I wear it Dad," Sandip had said resolutely, and then muttered under his breath, "It's a bloody nuisance, anyway."

At the severity of this opinion, Hiren had, as always, started to sermonize him on the disregard for his own tradition and culture; but this time he hesitated, looking at Sandip's face, he knew that his son was right. There was nothing that either of them could do or say now that would change the way things were, and the thread, in its hapless role would be a mere reminder of the futility of their lives together.

When the trouble began at school, Anjali and Hiren thought it was because they were neglecting their child. They began to bring home gifts for him each day, computer games and a Play Station, snazzy t-shirts and music CDs. They thought that this would keep him occupied; he was a teenager after all. But the incidents continued, his grades at school dropped considerably and the teachers began to complain that he had been missing from classes.

Anjali reacted badly to all this; her childhood had been a strict regime of studies and achievement. There had been no time to play, no time to squander on pleasurable activities. After the incident with the girl, Anjali had taken things into her own hands and had forbidden Sandip from all social outings and activities; things which by now he had become excessively used to.

One evening, as Mr Mukherjee cooked dinner and Anjali sat reading some research on the computer in their unkempt living room, they heard their son, who was supposedly studying for his exams, come downstairs. Anjali looked up over her glasses as he came into the room.

"Where are you going?" she asked nervously as she saw him pulling on a blue raincoat. There was silence, not unusual for most interactions between mother and son nowadays.

"Answer me," she screeched, her voice rising, edged with anger, at which Mr Mukherjee came out of the kitchen, a ladle in his hand with which he had been stirring the *daal*. A strong smell of roasted cumin wafted after him. He looked at his son; his young handsome face tight and closed, his wife looking furious, on the verge of an outburst.

"What's happening?" he ventured quietly, the *daal* dripping down the side of the ladle like a yellow snake.

"Where are you going son? Is there anything we can get you?" he asked delicately.

The silence continued until Anjali broke it.

"Tell your father at least you despicable child. Where do you think you are going?"

Her face distorted as she shouted, and momentarily Mr Mukherjee stepped back in himself, almost petrified to see the woman who stood before him, the girl he had married, who he had nurtured in his own home. He looked at her now, the long plait was missing, her hair was now cut short, and at the front of her head it was thin and sparse. She wore trousers and a shirt that hung loosely over it. She could have been a man; all the allure of the woman who he had met in Kolkata had left her.

What had happened to her, he thought, his mind racing across all the unremarkable years in which he had been stuck in a cubicle on the fifth floor, whilst his wife had turned into this stranger?

As she ran towards Sandip, an arm raised to hit him, Hiren threw himself between mother and son. Dropping the ladle, he took hold of his wife's arm, and she cried tears of rage as their son turned around and left the house.

That evening they did not eat dinner. The half-cooked *daal* stayed congealing on the stovetop, the smells dissipating into the curtains, the carpets and upholstery. They sat together in silence and waited for Sandip to come home. When at three am they heard the sound of his drunken laughter echo hollowly down their street, his keys jingling in the front door, Mr Mukherjee led Anjali up to their bedroom. That night, for the first time in years, he held his wife against him as she cried into the dawn. That was when Hiren Mukherjee decided that he would retire, that was when he knew that sometimes expected roles are reversed, and he was meant to be at home. This was indeed his calling.

The house was dark as the taxi pulled up in front of it. The sullen driver pocketed his money and drove off in a hurry to leave the lacklustre neighbourhood. The box with Mr Mukherjee's belongings lay against the pavement, waiting outside its new home. The gate creaked a welcome as it opened onto the front patch of garden, wild and unkempt. He noticed an old bicycle of his son's leaning against the front wall. Why on earth did they still have it? He looked at it forlornly, hugging the box against him, reluctant to go inside the house, knowing that this was it; tomorrow he had no escape, nowhere else to go.

The phone rang from inside, hollow against the emptiness of the rooms. He did not hurry to answer it; he waited and took his time, taking the keys out from his pocket and slowly fitting them into the lock. As the door opened, he heard a message being left on their answer machine, curt and static, a voice without a body without a name.

He switched on the light and suddenly looked around at his home, appalled. It was such a mess, there were clothes and shoes lying across the stairs and along the hall; a pungent odour shrouded him as he closed the front door; the smell of a house that was unaired, unhappy, and desperate to be cleaned. He left the box at the door and wandered towards the living room where he switched on a lamp. A yellow light spilled over everything, Anjali's papers strewn across the table, cups with leftover dregs of tea, a plate with a half-eaten slice of toast left from the morning, or perhaps the previous morning. He stepped towards the answer machine, the message flashing, anxious to be heard. He pressed the play button, waited for all the beeps and whistles and screeches to finish before the message began. It was Anjali. Her voice was dry and tight.

"I will be late tonight Hiren. You can cook dinner since you will be home early. Make sure you pick up Sandip from his football club at eight."

There was quiet after this, no goodbye, and no words of endearment, just a static silence as Mr Mukherjee stood and looked around himself. His work had just begun.

Computer Moshai
(The Computer Teacher)

Tapashi awoke earlier than usual. The hands of the clock next to her looked tired in the pallid light of dawn. Tugging down the hem of her nightdress she searched for her slippers on the cold stone floor. As she wound her grey hair into a tight knot she could hear her husband grunting from the room next door. Usually she felt nothing when she woke; she felt no excitement, no urgency to start her morning ablutions. After all, Shamir was retired, and even though he rose at four every morning to do his painfully contorting exercises, he demanded nothing from her at that hour. Later perhaps, he would meekly ask for a cup of tea, but usually at this time he was best left to himself.

Today, Tapashi felt a faint stir in the pit of her stomach. The same kind of slight, elfish quivers she had felt when she had been pregnant with their son Rahul; the same small jumps and ripples in her abdomen, which had so excited and comforted her then. Now in her early sixties she knew this was no pregnancy, but perhaps it was a sign that the mundane life around her was at last beginning to stir.

Today was Tuesday and for the last couple of months Tuesdays would no longer be like any other day, stifled in the confines of routine in their three bedroom flat off Hazra Road; no cooking the same old dishes for lunch, and certainly no squabbling with Gauri the servant girl. She had even stopped snapping at Shamir and was once again, however briefly, the amiable Tapashi he had married over thirty-five years ago.

Tapashi took less time in the bathroom today; fewer moments scrubbing the rough heels of her feet and the dark circles around her elbows with the pumice stone. She rubbed mustard oil hurriedly into her skin the sharp pungent smell waking her senses. She poured cold water over herself from the bucket, and as she stepped out of the bathroom, she wrapped a red striped *gamcha* around her upper body and padded into the early morning shadows of their bedroom.

The diaphanous material of the *gamcha* clung to her wet body, enhancing the contours of her full figure as she stood in front of the mahogany dressing table, a gift from her father at their wedding.

She frowned critically at the dripping reflection in its three angled mirrors. Her neck was still smooth, yet her face above it seemed to have aged. There were wrinkles where she least expected them, mapped out under her large almond eyes and at the corners of her full mouth, like reminders of the many smiles that had once flitted across her face. She had once been attractive, not beautiful, but striking in a rather unassuming way. Now her waistline showed the folds of age and her legs seemed to want to buckle under her with the increasing weight of her body and the newfound aches of rheumatism.

As Tapashi reached for the pot of pale pink sandalwood powder she sighed; at the thought of her aging body and the loneliness of their life on Hazra Road, but also at the distance from her beloved son Rahul who now lived in New York. As she patted the velvet puff around her breasts she wished she could visit him as he kept promising her in his emails.

Shamir came in from the adjoining room. His upper body was bare and there was a resigned slant to his once wide shoulders; now they were soft and effeminate. His eyes squinted into the semi darkness of the room as he saw his wife standing almost naked in front of the mirror. He turned to leave as was expected of him; nowadays they barely touched or spoke unless it was absolutely necessary. Today though he hesitated and watched her covertly from the corner of the room.

He saw her lips moving almost imperceptibly, as if she was whispering to the three reflections before her, and then he heard her sigh. The hush of air from her lips rode across on the cloud of talcum powder until it reached Shamir. He smelt the sweet heady scent of sandalwood, a reminder of the distance they now felt between them.

He saw the dripping red *gamcha* drop to the floor as she bent to pick up her petticoat; her breasts swung low and vulnerable, wrinkles faintly puckering the edges. Her stomach sagged from the traumas of childbirth and now with age, yet to him she looked so malleable, so tempting, so lost, almost like a child.

There were times, not unlike the present, when he had surprised her and she had giggled delightedly as he had pulled her towards him. Now the *gamcha,* which had once been the root of so much passion, stood as a sentinel in red, warning Shamir off: 'No trespassing', it seemed to say. Their home now stood quiet testimony to a past, which had slipped through their fingers, like sand. Tuesdays seemed to be their only reprieve.

As Tapashi bent to pick up the freshly ironed sari and blouse, she startled at the sight of Shamir in the doorway. She grabbed at her clothes, and he flinched, at the glare in her eyes and the outrage on her face.

"I was looking for the *gamcha*," he mumbled, embarrassed and almost scared.

"So take it," Tapashi said, clenching her teeth and looking towards the wet *gamcha,* now draped over the stool. "Take it and don't stand there and stare like some demented old man," she said fiercely.

So now, Shamir picked it up and fled to the seclusion of the bathroom, whilst Tapashi just stood there, despondently looking at her multiple reflections in the mahogany dressing table.

By mid morning the flat on Hazra was bustling with the sounds of cooking and cleaning. Gauri the maid sat hunched on the floor with the *boti* in front of her. The curved blade of the knife sliced through the uneven skin of the bitter gourds and the large slices of aubergines, which were to be dipped in batter and then deep-fried. Behind her, Tapashi was garnishing a plateful of mutton kebabs, which were her speciality. A pot of rice bubbled on the hob top ready to be strained.

There were three places laid at the eight-seated dining table today. The table that had seen so many friends and family sitting around its sharp Formica edges over lunches, dinners, birthdays, *poites*, and *pujo's*. Now usually, Shamir ate on his own at one end and after he had finished, Tapashi would organise the kitchen, serve the maids and then sit down to eat, alone, at the other end. This was the routine on every other day of the week, but today was Tuesday, and today the table was laid for three. Today was the day that Computer Moshai came to the flat on Hazra Road.

Almost twenty years ago, when Abhijit Sen's parents bid him farewell, they were convinced he would achieve great wealth and success in the US. But then four years later, just after completing his degree, their son returned.

At first his parents had felt proud that unlike most young people who never looked back once they had left, Abhijit had decided to return to the land of his birth, but soon they began to rancour as his contemporaries sent home huge sums of money from abroad, whilst their own son settled down quietly to a job as a computer salesman in a small software firm in Dalhousie.

As each month went by they recognised that the professional prospects for their son were diminishing, as were his prospects of marriage. Uncles and Aunts sympathised with his parents and lectured Abhijit on his lack of ambition and his need to take on more responsibility. He listened in silence, rarely contradicting anyone although he began staying away from home as much as possible, spending time in coffee shops in Golpark, and hours on a dusty lakeside bench.

He had met Shamir and Tapashi as friends of his parents at a musical gathering at the Birla Academy on a rare occasion that Abhijit had allowed himself to be dragged along. He had started talking to them, relieved to find a corner away from his parents. During the course of their conversation, Abhijit found himself offering to go and help the elderly couple with their computer, which it seemed, had been sadly neglected ever since their son had left home. They spoke proudly of their son, Rahul, about how successful he was as a Banker in a very desirable US firm.

"He works on the eighty third floor of the World Trade Centre," Shamir had said to Abhijit, with awe in his voice.

Abhijit had never been up the Twin Towers. In fact, he barely remembered doing much in New York except pass through to get the Amtrak on his way to Pittsburgh, where his college had been based. He nodded his head in appreciation, something it seemed he had done a million times since returning to Kolkata. He was used to this by now; the questions about his return, and his own vaguely whispered answers, followed by a full description of the son who was doing so well in New York, or Washington, or even the back yards of Arkansas.

Abhijit just listened quietly. It seemed that he knew more about the Indian youth in America then he did of those who lived in Kolkata. Like himself, they remained in the shadows of those who had left, forever the audience to their glorified lives.

Later, he had found himself seeking out time to go and visit Shamir and Tapashi in their Hazra Road flat. At first, he had tentatively gone and dusted the old computer and literally cranked up its tired innards to get it going. As Shamir and Tapashi had looked over his shoulders, he had opened out a whole new world to them, a world where they could not only see New York, but most of all, connect to their son.

Rahul had not been very good at phoning, or writing to his parents in the past, and although they had never complained it had been a quiet ache in their lonely old hearts. On the Internet, things were different; Rahul found it easier to write impromptu. To their delight, he was able to tell them small details of his life which they yearned so much to hear, like what colour shirt he was wearing at that exact moment and what he had eaten for dinner the night before. He talked about his work, the demands made on his time and the weekends he spent watching baseball or visiting friends. Once he even mentioned that he was meeting a girl for dinner that night and Shamir and Tapashi had immediately made Abhijit write back many questions: Who was she? Was she Bengali? What did she do for a living?

Abhijit had complied quietly, writing out the sentences dictated to him word for word. He felt awkward about Shamir and Tapashi's discussions over his shoulder; they seemed to forget, that he was sitting there, listening. He thought of his own parents, and the desperate photographs of girls which they thrust at him every time he sat down. He felt himself envy Rahul's freedom to choose his own life; the people he met, even the food he ate, whilst he Abhijit, just sat here as voyeur to a life which could have been his own.

Soon the couple became dependent upon Abhijit's visits on Tuesday afternoons. Tuesday was the day his work brought him to the area around Hazra, visiting schools and recommending new software. It was easy for him to take a long lunch break and drop by. It felt good being made such a fuss of, to feel so important, and for once be depended on for something. His own parents now openly complained about his meagre income, and his lost years in the US. His mother had wept when she heard her nephew in Boston had just had another son.

"Why could that not be you?" she had cried over Abhijit as he tried to eat his dinner. He continued to eat in silence.

"We would have been happy with anything. You could have married anyone, done anything but you decided to come back here. For what? To lead us to our early graves?" she asked, her body shaking with anger and disappointment.

Abhijit had left his dinner unfinished at the table, yet again.

So for Abhijit the flat on Hazra was like a getaway, a safe haven. Over the weeks Abhijit not only got to know Shamir and Tapashi, not only appreciated their warmth towards him and the efforts they would go to for him on Tuesdays, but he also secretly enjoyed being part of Rahul's life.

In Rahul, Abhijit seemed to live the life that he had so whimsically let slip through his own fingers. He laughed at Rahul's anecdotes about office life in the Twin Towers. He was in awe when he read aloud the fact that whilst it was clear and sunny on the 83rd floor, down below on the ground floor there could be a snowstorm in full blast. He almost seemed to taste the jumbo sausages and baloney sandwiches that Rahul had for lunch, and he congratulated him when he was promoted to senior executive.

He sat in his chair, holding open the line of communication within a family which was not his own. He was there when Tapashi clapped her hands with childish delight when Rahul wrote to say he would send them tickets to visit New York; or when Shamir inadvertently clutched his shoulder when he read about how Rahul had been mentioned in a *New York Times* article about up and coming young executives. Abhijit lived it all on those Tuesday afternoons in the flat on Hazra Road.

Shamir had changed into a fresh pair of starched white *Kurta Pyjamas* and had washed his hands in anticipation of lunch. The smells from the kitchen had been titillating his nostrils for some time now. As the doorbell rang Tapashi rushed out from the kitchen, getting to the door even before Gauri could get to it. He had noticed how light his wife's footsteps would become when the hour approached, he had heard snippets of her singing from the kitchen as she organised the food and laid things out. Momentarily he thought about her swaying breasts again, as he had seen her this morning.

Tapashi opened the door. Abhijit stood there, dark and sweaty. September still could be quite hot in the afternoons. The humidity was overwhelming, the pollution and traffic clamouring for attention.

"How are you, Mashi Ma?" he said to Tapashi as he bent down to touch her feet.

Tapashi smiled as she touched the top of his head in blessing.

"Fine, Fine. Come, come. Look at how hot you are. Gauri, take Dada's bag and bring him a glass of water will you. Just the way he likes it, half fridge half filter water."

Gauri came out of the kitchen wiping her hands on her sweaty cotton sari. She took Abhijit's bag feeling the handle sticky and hot. Abhijit slipped off his shoes and socks by the door, relishing the cool of the floor tiles against his overheated soles. In the bathroom, he splashed cold water over his face, and lathered his hands and face with the fresh bar of green Margo soap Tapashi had put out for him. He looked around, at the now familiar surrounds. He knew that on the windowsill there was a steel bowl of mustard oil, the yellow, viscous liquid dotted with floating bubbles after it had been dipped into with wet hands; the red *gamcha* drying on the back of the door; Shamir's old razor next to his tongue scraper, all neat and organized like the rest of their lives.

He felt a strange sense of belonging as he heard their voices from outside, Tapashi suggesting what should be served first, Shamir glad to agree with her. The fresh blue towel, left out for him next to the basin, smelt faintly of mothballs as he wiped his face and emerged into the living room.

"Come, son, come and sit," said Shamir as he plumped up the cushions on the sofa, making a comfortable corner for Abhijit.

"It still is so hot outside in the afternoons isn't it? How are things at work?"

"Fine Mesho," Abhijit replied between gulps of the cool water that Gauri had left for him on the side table. A small plate of sweets was placed beside it, soft white circles of Bancharam's best *mishti*. They looked tempting as they were meant to be and Abhijit was ravenous; breakfast had been a hurried affair that morning, escaping a new onslaught of admonishments from his mother.

Sitting in the comfortable cool living room of Rahul's parents, he felt at home and nurtured. Shamir talked to him about life, the market, and computers whilst Tapashi fussed around the lunch table, occasionally turning to smile upon the two men reclining in their corners. She was happy. Today she felt Rahul might tell her when exactly he wanted them to come and visit him. She had already started packing her cases in her mind. She would have to fish out all their old woollen gear, the coats and jackets and shawls she had carefully packed away so many years ago.

"Come for lunch both of you," she announced.

Their conversation about the latest IBM prices was cut short as Shamir smilingly hustled Abhijit to the table.

"Today, dear, you seem to have worked wonders," said Shamir, looking fondly at his wife, Abhijit's presence giving him the courage to do so. Tapashi avoided his gaze, but a faint smile twitched the corners of her mouth as she pulled out Abhijit's chair for him.

"Abhijit, did you know these kebabs are Rahul's favourite? When he was little he would steal as many as he could from the fridge to have as a midnight feast," Shamir added pushing the plate of Kebabs towards his guest.

Abhijit laughed politely. He felt guilty sometimes, taking Rahul's place at the table, biting into all Rahul's favourite food. He knew he was just a temporary fixture, till Rahul came back home or they went and lived with him. Then he, Abhijit, would have no other life to lead but his own. He felt like an impostor, desperately trying to fool both this innocent elderly couple and himself. Did he believe he was some kind of surrogate son to them? He was just 'Computer Moshai' to them, he knew. Shamir called him that affectionately sometimes, joking about how at their age they were taking tuition, from someone so young. He was just Computer Moshai to them, and always would be.

Lunch was grand as usual. The rice was light and fluffy, the aubergines fried perfectly crisp. Shamir was proud that the fish he had picked at the market was so fresh. He watched Tapashi eat, her fingers delicately curling around the mounds of rice, which she then tucked lightly into her mouth. She ate with him so rarely nowadays he had almost forgotten how she liked to chew the sweet bones and flesh of the fish gills, how she closed her eyes as she licked the sour chutney off the end of her fingertips. Abhijit ate fast and quietly. He let Tapashi and Shamir talk to him, giving only the occasional grunt in response.

It was almost three by the time they had finished lunch and had a round of *paan* to help digestion. They lounged on the sofas. Tapashi had helped Gauri clear away and had sent her home for the rest of the afternoon. She would make the tea herself today, whilst they sat around the computer. She hoped Abhijit would help her send her own personal message to Rahul. She meant to pass on a recipe for biryani, which he had asked her for last week.

She had spent a long time writing out the recipe in her delicate handwriting, and translating the ingredients into English with the help of an old A.T Dev dictionary. It was ready today, tucked into the folds of a diary, which they kept handy just in case they needed to note anything down.

Abhijit got up and switched on the computer. It would be early morning in New York now. Rahul would be munching on his croissant and drinking his Starbucks coffee on his way up the elevator of the WTC. He was usually keen to write to them first thing. Sitting here in their apartment on Hazra Road, his parents anticipated the moments they would soon snatch from their son's life. Through one sentence they would be connected, they would be together again.

The computer booted up. Abhijit knew all the passwords; after all he was the one who had set it up. He entered the mailbox. Shamir had pulled up his chair next to him; their shoulders rubbed together each time Shamir leaned forward to check on the computer's progress.

It was slow, lines were busy and it was almost half an hour before they heard the affirmative ping of connection. Tapashi, who had gone to the kitchen, was just putting the tealeaves into the kettle when she heard the now familiar sound and she hurriedly stuck down the lid and almost ran to be at Abhijit's side.

"Start with a hello and how are you," said Shamir eagerly to Abhijit who had already started to do so.

He knew that if Rahul were there he would reply back with his cheerful good morning in a matter of seconds. They waited patiently as the message travelled through the system across the cyber seas and straight through to Rahul's computer on his desk on the 83rd floor of the Twin Towers.

Hi Ma and Baba

Shamir and Tapashi almost held hands as the thrill of their son's words swept over them in the quiet of a Kolkata afternoon.

What are you doing Son? Shamir dictated eagerly
Have you had breakfast yet? Tapashi added

There was a pause; the air was thick with expectation. Abhijit could smell the closeness of Shamir's breath in his ear, edged with the heady perfume of *paan*; he could feel the warmth of Tapashi's hand resting on his shoulder. The silence was beginning to get unbearable when Rahul went into the inimitable chatter of his life in New York; the moment his parents, and now even Abhijit, waited for so eagerly,

The weather here has been great and in the mornings I feel a real buzz coming all the way up here. Today I am a bit tired though because last night I had Pranav round for a visit, and you know how tiresome that can be. It was unavoidable and I was glad it's over during the week so that now I can plan the weekend. I might go to Chicago to see Shrabani and Dev in a couple of weeks. Have you both heard from Dev's parents? They might be visiting in October and you could send some stuff I need over with them.

Ma what about that recipe of Biryani? I might try it out on Saturday night if some friends come over for dinner. I have invited Devika and some of her friends too. Remember Devika? I shall try and get hold of a snap and mail it over to you next week. By the way, I am serious about you both coming over to meet her in person. How about spring? I might be able to take some leave in April; we could travel around the US?

Abhijit felt the pride in Shamir's voice as Shamir read the email aloud to himself and to Tapashi, looking back mid sentence to smile at his wife.

"Have you seen how thoughtful he is Tapashi? We have done well with him I think!"

Tapashi nodded in agreement, as she looked straight ahead at the screen, almost as if she expected her son to appear there in front of her.

"Ask him more about Devika," she urged. "I have a good feeling about this girl. So what if she is non-Bengali. Nowadays, everything is acceptable, after all our son is a citizen of the world."

They urged him to write. To ask about what he had eaten the night before for dinner, when he planned to visit Kolkata, to tell

Rahul about the friends and family here who all asked after him. Tapashi fumbled with the neatly written recipe, ready to dictate, as the Computer Moshai continued to write, his fingers racing across the keyboard, trying to keep pace with the old couple's eagerness.

Ma you worry far too much about what I eat. I think I might need to go on a diet. Devika certainly thinks so. Actually, perhaps you can ask the computer chap you are using to help set up webcam. You know it's a great way of seeing each other and also calls are free.

Abhijit squirmed briefly at this direct reference to him; he felt small and unintentional, stuck in the middle of this family. Suddenly, he felt alone, and insignificant, just the chap at the computer and nothing else, after all, that was what he was. Why did he kid himself that he was more than a mere technician to Shamir and Tapashi? Why did he imagine he could fill Rahul's shoes?

Rahul would you like me to send you the recipe now? Tapashi asked Abhijit to write as her hand shook, ready with the paper.

Ma, make sure it is your particular recipe and not something from a cookbook. I like the one where you add the mint leaves remember? And all particular measurements please, I am still new to this cooking business, last week....

There was a sudden break in Rahul's flow.

The words from America fell silent, and in Hazra Road, a child cried in the distance and a faint clamour of evening rose like a mist from the streets below. A bell rang from a distant temple, and the hollowed sound of an evening conch shell accompanied it. Somewhere, a fruit seller hawked his wares undecidedly as dogs barked to announce his passage through the streets. From the nearby *ghat,* the steady pounding of cloth against stone offered percussion to the evening's symphony.

"What happened?" Shamir said, concerned. "Is everything okay with the computer, Abhijit? Why did it cut off so suddenly?"

Abhijit tapped a few buttons and then decided to write back.

Rahul, what happened? Called away from your desk by someone? We are waiting to hear more from you.

The screen flashed momentarily. A few hurried words appeared in the middle of the page.

Have to go. There has been some kind of an earthquake and we have to evacuate the building. Will write later…

The weight of Shamir and Tapashi's disappointment flowed over Abhijit. He shifted uneasily in his seat, and cleared his throat.

"Perhaps we can try in an hour or so after he gets back to his desk?" he said to the elderly couple who were rooted to their positions looking at the blank screen in front of them.

Still clutching the recipe which she had pulled out of the notebook ready to dictate to Abhijit, Tapashi went quietly to the kitchen. Whilst she poured out the tea she watched Shamir sit quietly back in his armchair and reach for the television remote control. The BBC World Service news came on. Tapashi left the kitchen, drawn by the images on the screen. "What has happened?" she asked.

Abhijit and Shamir looked on in disbelief. What was happening to the place, which they had just been so closely connected to? Was this the real world now?

An anxious looking reporter asserted the news again,

A plane has just flown into the World Trade Centre in New York... Terrorist attack... Pentagon... The second tower has been attacked... The New York Fire Service has been mobilised.
The reporters repeated themselves all evening, the news getting worse, and the images more illusory.

Abhijit stayed over at the flat in Hazra Road that evening. He slept in Rahul's old room, illicitly comfortable away from the tensions of his own home. Shamir and Tapashi needed him, he reassured himself, an uneasy constriction clutching his chest as the images of the evening haunted him. They had been calm as he tried futilely to connect to Rahul's mailbox, as he phoned his apartment in Manhattan where the answer machine repeated a playful message in Rahul's voice. Abhijit had looked at both of them, unsure of what to say, wishing he could somehow run through those dust-hazed paper-filtered streets to rescue Rahul. Perhaps then he would have the real right to belong in their lives.

As dawn broke over Hazra Road and the crows nudged each other on the balcony, Tapashi and Shamir sat on the sofa together. Abhijit came out into the cold dawn-washed room, their pain almost palpable through their silence. He sat on the floor at their feet, his hands touching their gnarled, tired hands which were entwined in a painful clasp. As the tears finally came, he was there to shush them like he would a pair of young children; he held them and rocked them, and made them promises out of nothing.

The computer lay desolate and guilty in the corner. Perhaps this time Computer Moshai was here to stay.

The Release

Six days she sat staring out of the window at the bleak expanse of mud and dry grass which was their backyard. The yellow flowers of the laburnum tree drooped across the back wall, the poisonous seeds scattered over the square yard in blissful ignorance of their own venom. She did not speak to anyone, to neither of her eight-year-old twin daughters, and certainly not to her husband Mahesh. She just sat there, crumpled and angry, her lips tight, her forehead creased and flattened against the dirty glass like a defeated insect.

Ever since that evening when Mahesh had driven over to the police station and picked up her and his daughters to bring them home, Leela had refused to talk. In a strange way her silence helped dispel the dreary calm everyone in the household had managed to keep over the last few months.

Over the next few days she left the window only to cook and serve the girls' meals, again in heavy silence. No one knew when she ate, or whether she ate and when she went to bed. In the morning when Mahesh awoke she was as he had left her the previous evening, sitting and staring out at the miserable patch of land, which they had claimed as their back garden ever since they had come to England.

Mahesh had not asked her any questions as he signed the documents for her release at the police station. He had come as soon as he had received the phone call, her voice shaking at the other end, not offering him any explanations. A few times he had glanced nervously at her tear-stained cheeks and puffed-up eyes, her sari crumpled and worn, the hem wet from dragging through puddles, her long dark plait wretched and sagging across her rain-speckled black overcoat.

Each evening that week as he came home, he had looked hopeful as he climbed the steep concrete steps to the front door. He looked inside with a false expectant smile as his daughters sat in front of the television its grey light jumping off their wan faces, pleased to see him after yet another afternoon of silence. He dragged himself reluctantly to the kitchen at the back of the house where she sat mournfully at her usual place, her shoulders drooping more as each day went by, her fingers frantically twisting the border of her purple silk sari as if they were desperate to speak for her. She remained surrounded by a fortress of silence and soon he stopped trying to break through and went to find solace in the company of the children. He knew this was not just about Leela's experience that afternoon at the police station; it was about him and the brutal consequences of his mistake that had finally led their marriage down this path of despair.

When he came home from work that Friday, the sixth day since the incident, his wife and daughters had left.

*

Mahesh was an Engineer in a prestigious firm. He had moved to England three years ago with his wife Leela and his daughters Seeta and Anita. He had been offered the job whilst in India and had immediately taken the opportunity to come abroad. After all he needed the extra money the company was offering him to put towards the rather ambitious house he had committed himself to in Central Kolkata. Leela had followed him without asking any questions. When they had been married, arranged by their parents almost ten years ago, she had, like most good Bengali wives, given up any hidden ambitions or aspirations of her own in order to be at her husband's side. Not that Leela had ever thirsted for much; her upbringing and education were conventional enough for her not to make any plans for herself. Her destiny lay in the footsteps of her husband.

They had a good marriage, the kind of comfortable stage a couple reaches after nearly ten years of being together. Their daughters were well behaved and adjusted to their new surroundings well and Mahesh enjoyed the predictable warmth of the occasional intimacy with Leela. At work he was well respected and his mostly British colleagues were keen to offer him friendship and support in his first few months in a new country. Although he had never admitted to Leela, he had been apprehensive about the move at first. He was a man used to the conventional comforts of home and their life back in Kolkata had been good. He knew he had taken the offer because of the benefits of the salary. At the back of his mind, he looked forward to going back as soon as he had made enough money to live comfortably in the new house.

When he came home each evening to their rather old and dark Victorian semi, the familiar aroma of Leela's cooking reassured him. It greeted him at the doorway along with his daughters, their faces smiling and innocent, equally reassured to see their father home. As he took off his shoes and settled into the unfamiliarity of their lives he hoped nothing would change, except their location. Yet, things did change, sooner than he had expected, and the unfamiliar, which he had so far eluded, possessed his entire being.

After six months, they bought a small red fiat, which Mahesh with his international license was able to drive, at first hesitantly then more easily around the streets of South London. At the weekends his wife and daughters dressed up to go with him to nearby places, the park in Richmond where they were amazed at the herds of deer, over the bridge to Fulham where Mahesh got lost and then to the more comforting stretch of Tooting where he watched Leela as she would stock up on all his favourite vegetables and spices from the Gujarati supermarkets.

At home they would all eat around the television, their dinner spread out on sheets of old newspaper, watching the latest episode of East Enders. Although the house that he had rented was big, it was damp and dark in most places. The kitchen at the back was awkward to get to and upstairs a long corridor at the end of which was a cold pink bathroom divided the two bedrooms. At night the twins slept on a makeshift bed in their parents' room and when Mahesh was aroused by his physical needs he would nudge Leela to go and wait undressed for him in the spare room where he would join her.

Their lives fell into a comfortable routine, with Leela taking the girls to school in the morning after she had packed Mahesh some rotis and vegetable curry for his lunch. He had soon grown tired of the food he ate at the office canteen and Leela was more than happy to wake up early and make fresh food for him that he later on heated in the office microwave. He felt proud of his life when his colleagues eyed his delectable food whilst they sat and stared down at their own rather unappetising fare. At those times he felt he had done well by coming to England, by marrying Leela who so painstakingly looked after his every need. He never really questioned whether she was happy or not but assumed like most Bengali men in his position that she was content to just be by his side, after all she never voiced any complaints to him. Occasionally though, Mahesh found that he wished that Leela would perhaps show more signs of adapting to Western culture. To begin with he hoped she would swap her saris, which seemed so dreary and impractical in the wet weather for trousers and shirts. Leela refused though, playfully teasing her husband that he was trying to turn her in to a *Mem*, or English lady. Perhaps he would have been better off marrying one, she had said, confident that her banter would only make her husband smile. Mahesh didn't ask her again.

He watched the secretaries in his office, the young English women who seemed so comfortable and at ease in their suits and skirts. There was one particular girl called Denise who caught his attention. She had bright red hair and a freckled pale face, and would have been about 25 years of age. She wore tight silk shirts through which Mahesh was sure he could see the paleness of her nipples behind her lacy bra. When she walked she almost skipped on her three inch heels with pent up energy and her laugh was often heard above those in her secretarial pool. Mahesh found he often searched for her in the crowded canteen at lunch time, just to look, he assured himself, conscious of his fidelity towards Leela.

One day he bumped into Denise at the water cooler on his floor. He realised that she was as curious about him as he was about her. He was the only Indian male on their floor and looking at himself in the mirror he reckoned himself good looking with his long drawn-out eyes and high forehead. His lips were full and sensuous and back in India he had often been compared to the legendary film actor Uttam Kumar by his doting family. Denise smiled at him sweetly and he felt good. At this a twinge of guilt crossed his mind, just fleetingly before it disappeared into the recesses of the present moment. As she bent down to pick up her glass from the cooler he saw her trousers pull down her back revealing the upper half of her buttocks, tight and round with the thin taught skein of red nylon that was her thong. He had only seen underwear like this in lingerie catalogues and the occasional Hollywood movie which he forced Leela to watch with him sometimes late at night. He felt an unusual sense of excitement, and a few days later braved himself to go into a lingerie shop in their local mall and pick up a pair of black thongs. That night he made Leela wear them. At first she had hesitated, awkward at his request, but she obliged by putting them on and giggled as he looked so excited. She found them incredibly uncomfortable though and commented to him on how the English girls could walk around all day with a nylon rope sticking up their bum. She preferred her own comfortable full briefs, perhaps her outer wear looked uncomfortable but inside she knew she was at ease. Whenever Mahesh thought about Denise, which seemed to be more and more each day, the more often he got Leela to wear the thongs. She indulged him, not knowing what it was that he found so fascinating, innocent in her belief that her husband's whims were guileless.

One afternoon Mahesh met Denise for a drink. They went to a pub around the corner from their office, frequented by many of his colleagues. He wasn't a big drinker himself and was surprised when he saw Denise order herself a pint of Guinness. He himself sat nursing a small lager, watching her as she sipped from the generous pint glass the creamy froth hanging from her upper lip momentarily as her tongue flicked out to lick it off.

Denise lived by herself, she had been through a series of boyfriends but was now quite single and looking for the right man to come along. She said this as she stared up at Mahesh with her liquid green eyes, a coquettish slant to her lips. He was bewildered at how it didn't seem to bother her that he was married, that he had children and that she had so many more men in the office whom she could pick from. He was fascinated by her openness, her blatant sensuality which was so raw and uninhibited. She was almost like any of the bizarre alien creatures he saw in the National Geographic magazines, living a life so different to his own. She invited him to her flat which was just a short journey away from the office and Mahesh, at first hesitant, accepted her offer.

At lunch they started to leave surreptitiously from separate entrances and he would find her naked and waiting for him sprawled across her bed. He barely noticed the meagreness of her home, the pink curtains and chintz armchairs the rows of CDs lined up against the windowsill. At first he had wanted to just linger over the alienness of her body, as if he had been offered a treasure which was beyond his imagination. He marvelled at the pale taughtness of her breasts, the cherry shaped mole on her left thigh, the smooth hairless contours. He found himself comparing every inch of her to the familiar mass that was Leela's body. How could two women be so different, he had thought to himself as he thrust himself with abandon inside her as she yelped and screamed in ecstasy?

Back at home he began to make peculiar demands on the unsuspecting Leela. He insisted she shave her legs, something which she had never done before, never thought that it was necessary, but after a few times she had let the stubble grow back and Mahesh had found this worse than what it had been before. Sometimes he urged her to scream his name when he was inside her which embarrassed Leela very much.

"What kind of demands have you suddenly started making?" she asked incredulously.

"I should not be shouting out your name, are you not my husband? And what if our daughters hear us, *chi, chi*." she said and shook her head crossly as she put her nightdress back on.

Mahesh decided to spend a night at Denise's flat. He told Leela that he was on an office trip to York and would call her when he got there. In the evening after they had dinner of grilled chicken and salad over a small tea light on Denise's dining table, he called Leela.

"I have just reached," he lied as he watched Denise clear the table.

"How are the girls? Tell them Baba misses them," he asked as inside him a small tight ball of guilt nudged his heart, as he thought of Leela snuggling up with the girls in their bed. As he put the phone down he felt awkward in Denise's apartment, the photographs of her family on a beach holiday in Corfu lined her dresser and he was amazed by the amount of make-up she kept in the bathroom. Leela just had a lipstick and eyeliner he thought to himself. It was strange being anywhere but at home, even their old dank Victorian semi was home. He was beginning to regret staying out for the night, but as Denise stood in the door in a soft peach negligee he quickly forgot and reached out to nuzzle her bare shoulders. In the morning he was careful not to talk much as she dressed for work, he watched as she meticulously applied her make-up and transformed her face. It was almost as if she was two people at once, he thought uncomfortably.

Back in the office people had started to talk about Denise and Mahesh. It was obvious that they disappeared at almost the same time together, how they avoided each other unusually at work parties and meetings. Mahesh could see some of his colleagues stare at him as he came back from another clandestine lunch, his lunch box of roti and sabzi untouched and emptied into the office bin as he headed home. At times Mahesh thought he should stop himself, but Denise was always there enticing him with her wonderful green eyes and smooth white limbs. At home he had stopped making Leela do things for him in bed. In fact he had almost entirely stopped asking her to join him in the back room as he had done before, now he just slept there on his own saying he needed to stretch out, instead of huddling up with his family in one room.

The evenings away became more frequent and he tried to make up for it by taking the girls and Leela out a lot more on the weekends. One weekend he took them to a shopping centre near Croydon. It was near Christmas and the streets looked festive with the trees draped in sparkling lights. His daughters skipped along in front of them as they held bags of roasted chestnuts. Leela stopped and looked into each shop window amazed at the decorations. He indulged her and let her go into the shops she liked and smiled as she came out appalled by the prices compared to things back home. It was then that he saw Denise, her red hair piled up on her head, wearing a tightly-fitted black dress underneath the open-fronted red coat. She was with her mother it seemed, she looked familiar, a face that had stared at him from the pictures on her mantelpiece. They came towards Mahesh, relaxed and happy, guilt free women.

"Mahesh how are you?" said Denise smiling, her sparkling glossed lips parted suggestively. "This is my Mum."

"Lovely to meet you," said Denise's Mother as she looked approvingly at Mahesh

"Denise has told me so much about you. Sounds promising." She said with a wide smile, her breath tinged with cinnamon from the mulled wine held in a polystyrene cup in her left hand. She winked at him knowingly.

At that moment Mahesh was acutely conscious of Leela who had emerged from the shop she had been browsing in and was quietly stood behind him. His daughters were a few feet ahead giggling at a man dressed as Santa's elf passing out flyers for a sports shop.

He saw the look in Denise's eyes as she focused on Leela, he dared not look behind at her.

"This must be your wife Mahesh?" she said with a smirk of her moist lips as she stretched out her hand towards Leela.

"How nice to meet you"

Leela took Denise's outstretched hand hesitatingly. She looked up at Mahesh and he knew in that instant that she knew everything. Here in front of her was the explanation of all those evenings away, the separate rooms, the thongs and the shaved legs. Looking at Denise and her mother swan away he wanted to fall at Leela's feet and beg her forgiveness but she just looked at him and shook her head in disbelief.

"why?" was all she had said.

They drove back home in silence, where she had broken down and cried and then screamed about the hopelessness of their situation, about the years she had lost being his perfect wife. The girls held onto their mother's dishevelled sari, crying unknowingly, scared of their mother's anger and their father's guilty silence.

Mahesh found himself escaping to Denise's apartment in the evenings just so that he could be far from Leela's anger. Their adopted life in that Victorian semi which had been so close to being perfect, gradually fell to pieces, scattered regardless on foreign soil. It was on one such evening, whilst Mahesh lay on Denise's sofa, his head in her lap, that Leela had called him from the police station. His colleague's wife had given her Denise's number. She called him there and asked Denise who had picked up the phone, directly for him.

She had not explained herself to him, just asked him to come and get her and the girls. That was when the silence began.

On the sixth day after she had gone he found a letter from the Police Station waiting on the floor on the hard coir doormat. He opened it and read, his mind going back to the moment in which he had found her at the station, the dark kohl that rimmed her eyes dribbling down her cheeks to form muddy rivulets. The girls had looked scared too and it pained him suddenly to think of how he had ruined it all, how for his love of difference he had shirked off the mundane. The crime mentioned in the letter was a mistaken case of shoplifting. Mahesh sighed and put it aside.

Inside, the house smelt of Leela's cooking. The curtains in the living room had been drawn across and the lamps lit. His kohlapuri slippers were laid out at the end of the sofa just as they were each evening, expecting him, silently reminding him that he was home. In the kitchen he saw a plate next to the hob covered with some white kitchen paper. He lifted it and looked; aubergine fritters, a mound of white rice a small bowl of *daal* and his favourite chicken curry.

He looked away into the garden, the darkness casting deep shadows at the end, his own reflection in the window staring at him woefully. As he watched, the night sky turned from a deep inky blue to pitch black. He could barely see the outline of the laburnum tree where last summer the girls, sun blotched and bruised kneed, had climbed up and hung a silver wind chime. The phone rang from the depths of the house. He saw himself start, his tired features contorted and then dropped. He knew it was Denise, he could almost hear the silkiness of her voice, her slight lisp, the pinkness of her lips held against the receiver. In the deep silence after the phone stopped ringing he pulled out a kitchen chair and sat down to his dinner. The wind chime tinkled gently on the laburnum tree.

Amongst other things

When Shonali returned to Konnagram it wasn't raining. In fact it hadn't rained for over a year. The skies seemed angry with resentment of the heat that had sapped the strength out of all living beings. It was a manic heat, vengeful and mean, leaving no one untouched. The air was thick and humid, wrapping itself around the suffering population, their limbs slow and sluggish under the weight.

The taxi driver who had brought Shonali from the airport in Kolkata refused to take her further beyond the Hooghly bridge. He looked back at her dolefully, his dark skin almost purple with the heat inside his yellow cab, the once red velvet seats foetid and black with the sweat of all his passengers.

"I won't get any passengers to come back" was his explanation as Shonali counted out his fare and fumbled with her baggage.

He looked ever so slightly guilty about leaving her at the corner of the street, alone with her bags and suitcase. He thought she looked troubled and her angular face and hooded eyes were weary and absorbed in thought. The corners of her wide mouth twitched occasionally, almost unsure whether she was going to smile or cry. Momentarily he nearly gave in. Konnagram was a place with an uncomfortable reputation for thieves and scoundrels. What would a young woman want here on such a hot lonely afternoon! As he pondered over this thought briefly, a rabid dog looked out of one of the dark alleyways that led into the town. One look at the pus-ridden limbs, the blue filmy eyes stuck together with unbridled infection and the bared fangs was all he needed to decide against offering help to Shonali. He was gone, in a puff of dust like a cowardly Lone Ranger.

Shonali looked around. The diseased dog limped away to lie underneath a *Peepal* tree which offered some shade. A travelling mendicant wearing just a small grey loin cloth lay on the stone base built around the tree. His hair was knotted and gnarled, almost meshed with the trailers that drooped from the branches above him. For one brief moment it looked as if he had grown into the tree. His trident and begging pot were tucked beneath his small bundle of cloth whilst he slept peacefully. Shonali sighed, suddenly feeling tired with the weight of the journey. Whilst the taxi brought her through the city she had been alert with noise, the shouting, the clamouring and honking of traffic. She had felt like a clockwork toy, rattling with wound-up energy. In the relative quiet here at the edge of Konnagram, the key had finally done its last turn. Her energy gave way to a leaden weight.

So does no one ever escape from Konnagram? Shonali thought to herself as she stood there. Did no one ever leave the winding alleyways and claustrophobic huddles of this town? Would she herself ever be able to escape from its clutches once she was swallowed again into its sordid depths, its hollowness, its brooding mysterious sorrows? Once, long ago, she had visited the town, a few weeks one summer when her poor suffering mother felt a strange need to see her neglected ancestral home. Although it had been a fleeting few weeks the place had never let go of its hold on her. However far she went, the house drew her towards itself, like an errant child to its patiently waiting mother.

The memories had faded though, her mother's face, her tinkling sad laugh, the crumbling house, the strangely stirring smell of cinnamon when it rained and the peculiar people who lived within.

She remembered the cracked dry face of Kamini Mashi her Grand Aunt, sitting in her rusty lopsided wheelchair cackling away at nothing and scaring the servants with her whimsical demands. Crazy Kamini Mashi, toothless and suffering with the burden of her own past. She remembered the house with its endless circling balconies, its half hanging rooftop gardens where she had caught nearly a hundred ladybirds in a jar. They had died later, when she left the jar on a scorching windowsill by mistake. They lay on their backs, sizzled and suffocated in the glass hothouse which she had offered as their home.

A glass palace which had become their tomb.

Then there was Malati the servant girl who she had played with. Malati with the long braids and puckered old lady's face; spindly legs and budding breasts. Malati, with whom she ran off to the *pukur* to collect spiders and belching pond frogs. Later with algae stained green feet they would creep giggling into the food cellar to steal pickled mangoes and tamarind chutneys to savour at leisure in their rooftop hide away.

That summer had been almost twenty-five years ago, and Shonali had never returned since. Now she asked herself what she had come back for, to a house which she had inherited from this demented Grand Aunt who was childless and grieving for years within its doomed walls. She stood there uncertain of her next move, not quite ready to venture into the future which lay before her, until she saw a rickshaw which she hailed.

"Praan Bari," she said to the rickshaw puller's impassive features as he helped her lug her case close to her feet on the battered tin ledge which served as a footboard. The seat was covered in a shiny plastic beneath which she could see the bright colours of a familiar pattern. He pulled the rickety wooden frame over her head, shading her from the heat, the side flaps loose and grimy in contrast to the newness of the seat. It had been years since she had been in one of these contraptions.

In London, where she had lived for the last ten years, rickshaws were no longer an alien concept. She had spotted a rather boxy but suave version on a Sunday afternoon in Soho, polished metal with red leather seats. The rickshaw puller, a rakish student, carefree and full of life as he whizzed past amused tourists and closed- faced Londoners. Edward was with her then, and had asked her if she fancied a ride. He wouldn't mind a ride himself. But that was Edward, as usual besotted with anything to do with the Orient. He was desperate to go to India to see the real thing, but she had kept putting him off, alarmed by his enthusiasm which made a mockery of her own lack of passion. In those days, he was so much more spontaneous, but then so was she, in those days, before it all fell apart.

The rickshaw puller here in Konnagram was a wasted soul, his face weather- beaten and ragged with the trials of making a living in this treacherous town. When Shonali mentioned her destination to him, she was sure she saw a flicker of interest in his eyes, a slight movement of those leathered facial muscles. Did he know who she was? Perhaps he knew why she was here?

She had called Edward from the airport, the line was crackly and his voice sounded so distant and faint and worried.

"Shonali," he slurred, "Where are you? I was so worried when your school called to say you had left early?"

His silence trembled as he waited for her explanation. She had been cruel to him, she thought, left him so thoughtlessly, but she had to get away and fast. Something inside her ached as she told him that she was fine and that he should not worry. Should he? The questions between them crept unsaid across the telephone lines. Now he would be in bed at this hour, lying amongst the crisp white linen sheets in their house in South London as the grey clouds gently woke him. She thought of his ruffled chestnut hair, his dark eyes and she almost wished she could go back. But there was just silence between them now, as it had been for the past year ever since she had lost their child in a cold London hospital room, ever since she thought she could never love him as she had done before.

A bubble of silence surrounded their lives now.

A few stray goats lay in the shades of the dusty trees, looking exhausted, their tongues hanging out, their abdomens distended and heaving as they breathed deeply.

Shonali held onto the sides of the rickshaw, peering through the flaps to see whether she could recognise anything at all after so long. An aching fist clutched her heart, the fear of what she was doing and where she now was. Everything looked strangely familiar and yet at the same time so alien. Was it she who had changed or was this place so ageless and monotonous? The rickshaw puller snuck a look back at her a couple of times, his shirt drenched, his face oily and red with the exercise. She could see the taught muscles in his legs as he pushed up and down, down and up, rhythmically, on the stiff untreated pedals, his feet were bare, the soles as hard and leathery as the soles of hobnailed boots.

They turned left and right, into emaciated gullies where the overripe stench of narrow drains made her cover her mouth to stop from gagging. She could hear a child crying as they passed an open window and a woman's high pitched shriek from another. Two old men sat on chairs with their feet dangling in a tin pail of water, like dying reeds desperate to soak some water to live on. The uneven road jolted her and shook her and a couple of times her handbag nearly slipped out from her lap, but she held on tighter, her fingers wet with perspiration her wedding ring shining ominously on her swollen middle finger.

Finally, the rickshaw puller swerved and stopped and with a sudden clasp on his breaks he jumped off and stood holding the handlebars almost steadying his mechanical horse from the momentum of the chase. In front of them loomed the house, which Shonali recognised immediately, even though it had changed, was more dilapidated, crumbling and sore with age, oozing neglect. The big difference was that this was hers now, her very own, with a twist of fate one childless soul leaving it for another. A century of darkness loomed over the building lending it an uncanny air of sombreness. Her womb ached, twinged momentarily and then laid still, its emptiness acknowledging what lay before her.

The front gate where they had stopped, once green as she remembered, swung eerily half open on its hinges; eaten away over the years by the wind and the rain and the insatiable woodworm. It kept nothing out, it protected nothing, just a meaningless slab of chewed wood pretending to be a gate.

A little boy of about five or six skipped out of the house. His brown, weather-beaten legs and arms painfully thin beneath his blue check shirt and khaki shorts; his hair well-oiled, well-groomed, his teeth shining white as he grinned at Shonali's attempts to keep open the groaning green gate.

"Who are you?" he asked as he looked her up and down.

Shonali suddenly felt embarrassed by her own appearance. Since she had left London which was almost twenty hours ago she had not even once brushed her shoulder length dark hair. Neither had she applied any make-up, her face suddenly felt naked and dirty in front of the little boy's curious gaze. His eyes sparkled with hidden mirth as she squirmed and searched for the right words to identify herself. Who was she? The new owner? The forgotten niece or the neglectful daughter who had married an Englishman? How much did he know and what did he expect? She tried to brush back a few wisps of loose hair behind her ears, knowing it was futile; her lips felt dry and chapped, her skin papery. She hesitated whilst he stood there, a small sentinel at the gate forbidding her entry until she had correctly identified herself.

"I am Shonali," she said softly bending over him so that she smelt the rawness of soap and coconut from his skin. Before she could say anymore the little boy lifted his head and shouted out towards the loose green shutters of the house,

"Ma! Ma! It's Shonali Mashi!" And with glee he skipped off shouting for his mother. Shonali's heart ached as she watched him, his slim waist tightly cuffed in a wide leather belt holding up his shorts which obviously had at some stage belonged to someone else, someone with a much wider waist.

The rickshaw driver put down the last of her luggage touched his fee in gratitude to his forehead and drove off again, leaving Shonali once again standing alone but perhaps this time not unknown, in a place where she had once thought she belonged.

On a grey morning that February Shonali found herself with her head half immersed in the toilet bowl. Outside it was a pallid wintry day, the skies hastening by in the blustery cold. Their small house was just about beginning to heat up since Edward had left for work at seven that morning. It was still dark when he left, quietly washing himself, not wanting to wake her whilst she burrowed under the mound of covers on the bed. He usually brought her a cup of tea, left it quietly at her bedside and kissed her goodbye at the same time. She could smell the cold metallic odour of his suit then, the waft of long travel on the underground jostling amongst similar smelling commuters.

This morning the tea was left untouched on her bedside, the warm earthy colours of the liquid now slowly discoloured in the dainty floral mug that Shonali had once picked from a stall at Portobello market.

At first the pain was in the lower back, sharp and sporadic, she held her breath each time it knifed through her body. As the morning went on and she heaved and twisted her heavy seven month pregnant body from one side to the other under the covers, the pain slowly stretched its fingers to her entire abdomen. She retched painfully as she sat up and tried to reach for her bathrobe flanked across the end of the bed. Her eyes adjusted to the light seeping through the blinds, cold and icy like her pain. Her entire being ached. From her head to her shoulders, her breasts weighty and sore stretching out of her chest, her stomach far distended beyond her dreams, her ankles tight and swollen. As she ran clumsily for the bathroom, a surge of nausea gurgled upwards from within the body which Shonali no longer believed to be her own. She had no time to reach for the light switch to dispel the darkness, just enough time to fling her head into the toilet bowl and let out a painful agonising streak of yellow bitter bile.

She stayed there, retching and crying alternatively all through the morning. Outside the milkman with his two finger-smudged bottles rang the bell and left his delivery on the doorstep. The quietness of mid-morning fell over the neighbourhood, houses shuttered, children in school the elderly stagnant in front of their television sets. Shonali stayed next to the toilet.

The phone rang in the living room, echoed through the emptiness of the house, down the stairs, across the narrow hall with the large-eyed print by Jamini Roy on its right wall, the television cold and dead at this hour. The kitchen sink dripping drearily as it looked out upon the barren square of muddied winter grass which was the garden, still and bereft of life.

At noon Shonali, empty and hoarse got up, pulled around her shoulders the blue fleece nightgown which was all she seemed to want to wear nowadays and with a great force of will climbed down to the kitchen. She looked at herself in the hall mirror as she passed. Never quite happy with the way she looked, now she glared at her image, almost clawed at her skin to rid itself of its sickly grey, a fleck of saliva hung morosely from her wet hair. As Shonali sat down at the kitchen table she saw the machine flashing a message on the answer phone, she looked away. She knew it would be Edward, kind, gentle Edward, with his soft caressing fingers his silken voice, the voice she had fallen in love with on Magdalene Bridge on a crisp October morning in Oxford as he called her name across the breeze. Now she didn't want to pick up the phone to hear his message, she resented his normalcy whilst she sat here sick and wretched and bloated, no longer the Shonali who she knew he missed.

He had wanted this baby so much, from the day she told him that she was pregnant he had soared with enthusiasm and energy. Curtains, blankets, nappies and baby products were all stacked neatly in the little cupboard in the spare room where their baby would come to live. He whispered to it at night, his breath hot and soft against the soreness of her taught belly; names which sounded cold and alien to Shonali's ears, like Max and Emily, Brian and Jane. Names which she knew she should by now have taken to her heart, as much as Edward was happy and open to adopt any name she preferred. But she was silent, ominously silent, which he put down to her constant sickness and hormones.

One evening he had brought home a bunch of flowers for her, to cheer her up. She sat staring wearily at them as he arranged them in a vase, looking smiling towards her, then sitting down to nuzzle her shoulder whilst his hands rubbed her bump. Shonali felt the urge to scream, to tear at Edwards face, stamp on the flowers and throw down the sickening yellow vase on the floor. She felt trapped underneath his warmth, his happiness, a feeling she had never thought she would confront ever since they had met three years ago, ever since she had decided to marry him, written to her family to tell them that she was marrying an Englishman called Edward.

Her mother's sad letters had gone, unheeded into the wastepaper basket. Shonali's Uncle who lived in Leicester, a trembling retired English Professor had come reluctantly at his Sister's persuasion for the small civil ceremony at the Chelsea town hall, where Shonali had skipped down the steps in her tight white dress into the June air, holding Edwards hand tightly. She had rebelled against the sheepish angst on the face of her only present relative, her mood buoyant and soaring she had wrapped her arms around Edward and kissed him on the mouth, long and full, knowing that she made her Uncle squirm as he looked on.

He had avoided her at the after wedding party, swarming with their friends from Oxford and Edwards's family. He sat in a corner and had his plate of smoked salmon, skipped the main course of beef fillet in a peppercorn sauce and shook hands with her and left before the dancing began. She never heard from him again, but later that week after their honeymoon in Paris, as they sat and unwrapped the wedding presents in the living room of their home, she opened a package in which there was a beautiful red shawl with a black embroidered border. When Edward asked who such a lovely present was from, she lied and said it was from her friend Susan.

Now Shonali often opened her cupboard and brought this shawl out. Guiltily feeling its soft richness, smothering her face within the folds, evocative of the family she had so hastily thwarted. She dared not call her Uncle after how she had behaved at her wedding, but her heart yearned for the company of this stranger who was the only link she had with her past.

She felt a scraping in her belly, did the child know what she was feeling, and did he or she want to escape from the womb that held it so tightly in her body. How would it feel when it found out that its mother had no ties with her past? She was born of air grew in the solitude of air and now had taken on Edward's identity. Who was she and where did she belong?

The doorbell rang.

She heaved herself reluctantly up, hoping it wasn't her ever-so-kind and annoying neighbour who had already drawn up plans with Shonali about how they would share the childcare with her own two year-old son. She had even urged Shonali to put the child's name down for a school in the area, but Shonali dodged her whenever she asked her whether she had registered. How could she, when she could not even think of a name to give to the baby.

The outline of the person she could see through the frosted glass of the front door seemed to be familiar. She felt sick again, a surge that battered her insides like a ghastly wave. As she reached for the door, there was sharp pain in her back, a stabbing whilst she felt the baby kick her belly at the same time. It felt strange. She opened the door, the outline remained the shadowy outline, and a voice spoke through a black hole that was a mouth, in a language she did not comprehend. The pain wrenched her so hard she felt the floor and the walls rising up and closing in on her as she landed with a soft thud against them. Then there was darkness.

When she awoke she did not recognise the blue and white walls and strange steel furniture. It took a few minutes and a glance to her left out of the dark window that made her realise that it was a hospital room. The sheets covering her felt cold, her feet were freezing. As she moved, her body still ached but there was a strange lightness about her lower half. As she attempted to sit up, the door opened and Edward walked in. His face looked thin, his smile weak as he sat next to her and fumbled awkwardly for her hands. His lips kissed the papery coldness of her skin; she felt the rawness of his mouth, the warmth of his breath.

"Where is this?" she asked hesitant, her voice a low croak.

"It's the Chelsea Hospital. The neighbour brought you here after you collapsed at the doorstep." There was a small hint of apology in his voice, the way he looked down and pleated the corner of the sheet, his hands trembling. She waited.

"The baby's gone. It seems you had some internal haemorrhage, the placenta came out too soon." A tear fell onto her hand which he held in a tight grasp. She looked ahead not daring to meet his glance, afraid to let him see that she felt nothing, no pain, no sorrow, not even anger; just an empty distant yearning and a rush of loneliness that she was terrified to acknowledge. He sat there for a while, until the doctor and nurse bustled in, their stern faces showing the strains of their job. They gave her an injection and asked her how she felt. She did not answer, they exchanged looks with each other and then with Edward. They spoke to him outside after which he came into her more composed.

"The doctors say that you need to rest and I should get home. It's late. I have taken time off work and will see you tomorrow. I love you Honey!" He kissed her head and left, his brows clenched, wishing she would respond.

As the door closed she felt relieved. Her belly twinged again. Later she would learn that these were phantom twinges, like those felt after a limb had been amputated. Now she felt herself trembling, wishing suddenly she could feel that reassuring kick again. Tomorrow she would have nothing, she thought to herself, nothing to make her sick and nothing to make her cry. Then the tears came, in a loud gasp, awash with the misery and helplessness that she had felt for so long. In between her tears she suddenly realised that she hadn't even asked him what it was. Whether it was a boy or a girl that now lay on a cold steel slab within these very walls. The tears flowed freely now and she buried herself in her pillow until sleep overcame her.

His ever-present optimism was in the air as she entered their home after six days away. There were flowers upon the spotless kitchen table and she could smell cooking. The radiators were on to full blast and the air wrapped itself around Shonali's cold body, tugging and pulling her into the smiling hearth of their home. But

Shonali felt nothing. No warmth, no relief, not even any more tears. After her first outburst in the hospital, something else had died inside her and as much as she tried for Edward's sake to show her agony she could not bring the tears to her eyes. She felt like a fraud.

As Edward came in behind her with her bag from the car she heard him close the front door. A sudden panic gripped her throat, as if she was trapped in a warm cosy cell from which she could not escape.

"Would you like a cup of tea Honey? I'm desperate for one. Shall I put the kettle on?"

His voice feigned a cheerfulness which she knew must be for her sake, considerate as ever for her well being. He went ahead and put the kettle on, the gentle crackle and pop of the water heating up disturbing the sallow quietness of the kitchen. The morning sunshine filtered in through the windows that looked onto the back garden. A blackbird pecked gently at something in the trunk of the old yew tree that stood in the middle, patiently pecking, then tugging then pecking before it hopped onto its other foot and flew off. She wondered if their neighbours were up, Parisa and her son, her sulky husband who always ignored Shonali when he met her in the street. She had felt uneasy at first, even thought of mentioning it to her neighbour, but decided against it, she did not want to show she cared, that she felt snubbed, that she wished she could turn him around and shake him as he walked past. Edward was so different, she remembered thinking, so warm, so accepting. That night there had been a renewed vigour in their love making. She knew it was because she was uneasy, because she hated being ignored, even if it was by the unshaven husband of her Iranian neighbour. She needed attention, craved it, and lapped up all that Edward had ever offered her, and begged for more.

But now it seemed that, in the quietness of the morning in their warm kitchen, she had lost her appetite, her lust to be wanted, the need to fit in, to be admired, to be cherished. Like that lone blackbird on the yew tree, she needed to fly off somewhere different. She watched Edwards back, the gentle ripple of his muscles underneath his thin woollen jumper, the pale white of the back of his neck, his slim fingers as they busied themselves with teabags and sugar lumps. The way he made the mundane special as he always had, as he always would. She sighed, her fingers trembled as she felt the edges of the table mats which he had thoughtfully put out in front of her, afraid of staining the table surface. A wan smile crossed her face as she watched him now, her husband of three years, the father of her dead baby, the man she had given up her past for.

"Edward, do you remember the time we met? On the bridge in Oxford? In September?"

She didn't know what made her speak, something inside wanted to break the false pretence of cheerfulness that Edward was masquerading under. She wanted him to think of what was real, not the unreal, not the ephemeral nothingness that their life had slipped into over the past few months.

He turned around from the kettle where he had been pouring the hot water into their mugs and smiled wryly, the corners of his mouth drooping nostalgically downwards, his brows tensed gently over his eyes.

"Do you remember how you shouted my name over and over again until the people passing by began to stare and smile at us, as if we were two lovers in a climax scene of a movie?"

"I remember," he said, settling down at the table with his hands cupped around his mug glad that she had at last broken her mournful silence. He stared into the murky tea, as if it was the surface of a crystal ball, showing his past, his future, his present.

"I remember you were wearing that green dress, the one with the sequined collar." he said smiling.

"And you kept calling my name didn't you Edward? Until I heard you and turned back and saw you running towards me."

He chuckled gently as he looked into the past, a picture so perfect that both their memories together fragmented it into a glorious undying collage.

She continued talking, looking straight at him. She suddenly felt stronger, in control of their future, her future, his future. She knew what she needed to do, but first she must bring Edward to the surface with her, so that he could see clearly above the waves of unhappiness that both of them had suffered. Somehow she must throw him a log before she swam away to the other side, the side she knew she could not take him to with her. She had to leave.

Oxford had not been her first port of call when she had arrived here. Instead she had taken the bus from Heathrow on a bright Autumn morning to a city in the Midlands. A city which in all its grey drabness, its smoking cement chimneys, its mishmash of post-war architecture and alien looking inhabitants still looked exciting to her. She had just completed her Masters degree in Delhi, and was glad to have escaped the heat of the ensuing summer for the mildness of England. There was a thrill to being alone for the first time away from the clamour of the household in which she had grown up. Her parents had spent the last decade arguing with each other; each and every move of theirs was an irritant for the other. As an only child she felt the constant agonising pressure of their personalities bear down on her until she squirmed to be free. At the first opportunity she had applied to universities in the UK and was rather pleased that she was offered a position to do research at a not far from reputable institution. She was sad to say goodbye to Delhi and to her friends, many of whom had already left the city over the years since they had finished at school. Some had married and already had children who were already at school, some were in jobs in the city which was just beginning to see the signs of foreign investment. At a time when the future of India looked bright and prosperous Shonali decided to leave.

She settled down well to her new life. Her room in a shared household just outside the campus; the research fellows who came from all over the world; for the first time Shonali felt a sense of completeness, of having achieved something for herself and set foot into the wider world outside the precincts of Chittaranjan Park and their quietly festering household. A few years later her father died of a heart attack. She had already in her mind started to hate her parents for the melancholy they had caused her whilst she was at home and the freedom that they had almost forcefully driven her towards. She felt nothing when her mother phoned her tearfully to give her the news.

The company of her new friends satiated Shonali. She started to pretend that life at home was really as warm and exotic as people here thought it to be and the picture she painted of her family was one of regal splendour and contentment. The reality stayed hidden in a corner of her mind, only to come forth in the occasional lonely moment at night in her bed.

In the summer of her second year in England she visited Oxford with a group of her friends. It was then that she met Edward, in a pub, underground, where she saw him leaning over a glass of scrumpy at the bar.

It wasn't love at first sight as much as they would have liked to have thought. Much more than that, it was a sense of decision that they had both singled each other out from amidst the crowds that afternoon at the bar. As they had brushed against each other, jostled by friends, laughter ringing in their ears as their eyes had locked for a moment. They had spoken briefly, exchanged phone numbers and said awkward goodbyes. But they knew they would meet again, soon, whether in the cement valley of the Midlands or amongst the gleaming spires of Oxford.

He had called her almost immediately afterwards. The very next morning in hushed student halls on communal phones they exchanged pleasantries with undertones of an uninhibited passion. They had met almost each weekend, eating into their sparse student budgets as they travelled across the country to see each other, at first meeting for the afternoon, which extended into passionate Saturday evenings in unheated student digs.

Shonali felt that she had arrived. With Edward as her friend she had moved to another dimension of living. Each day she awoke with the joy of a life that she had chosen and rarely did she think of all that she had left behind. Her mother's letters to her each week pleaded with her to come home, now that her father had died she was alone, she needed to have Shonali by her side. Shonali loathed the emotions with which her mother wrote to her, she stopped answering her mail. She just tucked away the worn, blue aerogramme into the back of her volume of Shakespeare bought at a second hand shop in Warwick where she and Edward had spent the afternoon kissing on a wet October day.

Life was good for Shonali then, less complicated, yet not perfect. It now seemed a lifetime ago when she had met him, had loved him and used him as she played her part in a play of her own making.

Now she knew she needed to leave.

*

Three months later she was gone. She had packed her bags and left them in her cupboard. She handed in her notice at school that day, came home and took her bags to the airport. As she waited to board the aircraft she fumbled with the letter which she had received six months ago from her mother.

Your great aunt has left you 'Praan Bari'. The house you visited once as a child. I don't know what she was thinking, you obviously have no need for such ties with the past. I thought you should know about all that is yours. To take it is your will, the house will survive time.

She knew this was where she was going. Amongst all other things that had happened in her life, the efforts she had made to be something she would never be, this beckoned her like a monstrous figment of her past, haunting her memories calling her back to the beginning of a time that she had wished to forget and to ignore.

Jamun Reverie

"Jamani Kale, Kale Jaam," the dulcet tones of the *Kala Jamun* seller echoed through the afternoon hush, tempting people to awake when they heard his ditty about the flawless blackness of the fruit. But not a whisper from a bird or a rustle from the coconut trees replied from the slumber of the summer afternoon. Doors and windows remained shuttered and unblinking; dogs and cats panted gently in the shade, awaiting the evening. The *kala jamun* man took his usual route winding through the sweltering alleys, past the green waters of the pond towards the small cluster of houses that stood around it.

Awakened by the *kala jamun* cry, Bela opened one sleepy eye to look at the watch she kept underneath her pillow. Four o'clock, another half-hour before she would have to think of getting up. Her husband would want his cup of tea then whilst he sat in his faded green deck chair out on the downstairs porch. She turned over and watched the contours of her daughter's body rise and fall gently with a steady rhythm of deep sleep.

For a brief moment Bela felt disorientated. On so many similar afternoons she had awoken whilst her two youngest children Maya and Jai were still at college and her husband had only just retired.

But time had left all that behind. Maya was now married with two children and Jai had a good job in a marketing company, so he came home quite late. Now beside her the heaving contours were that of her eldest daughter Devi.

Earlier this afternoon Bela had catered to the tired appetite of Devi and her three lively children as they had arrived from Delhi for the summer vacation. She recalled how some years go when Maya and Jai returned from college they would both be famished, the usual steamed rice and mustard fish would disappear in minutes into their young mouths. In contrast, Devi's plate held smaller amounts. She was thoughtful as she ate, slowly moving the rice and *daal* around on her plate in concentric circles, before putting it in her mouth. Bela had been slightly irritated with her lack of interest in the food, but she knew her daughter was tired after the long train journey.

Devi's children had been high-spirited to start with running all over the house, shouting with delight as they came across familiar objects and corners, which they had not seen for a year. It was funny how they loved the familiarity of the place, the unchanging people, the swaying coconut trees outside, the cold stone floors. The little cupboard of porcelain figurines, the shelf with the old wood-bound tennis rackets, the faded windows that looked over onto the green waters of the *pukur*. After lunch their exuberance had faded a little and they had reluctantly dragged themselves upstairs to the large four-poster beds with the long side pillows. Bela could hear one of them giggle, as they now lay enveloped in a deep tired sleep. She smiled to herself as she thought of how the otherwise quiet house would now be filled with their laughter and mirth for the rest of the summer.

She thought of all the things she looked forward to doing for them, cooking their favourite dishes, encouraging their funny games and making sure they were comfortable during their stay. After all, her entire life had been devoted to looking after people, it was her sole occupation and she excelled at it. The first few years of her life had been spent in looking after her younger brothers and sisters. She was the eldest of sixteen offspring. Her mother, constantly weighed down with the duties of her growing household and her endless pregnancies had been compelled to leave the youngest children in the care of the eldest daughters. And so Bela had carried around number twelve on her hip whilst eleven and ten had followed her around everywhere. They knew they could depend on her for food and comfort more than from their forever ailing and exhausted mother.

Bela had married Keshav at thirteen, and had her first child at fifteen. The years that followed were full of the pain and joys of bringing up three children, of looking after her husband as he provided for her to the best of his ability. There followed years of childhood tantrums and ailments, and of striving to keep the household happy and content. They were years filled with the growing pains of daughters and sons and husbands and brothers, of bickering amongst servants and helpers and fisher women, of a constant flow of guests and friends and family who forever availed of Bela's hospitable nature. Lost in this endless surge of people Bela grew accustomed to forgetting about her own existence. She was part of everyone in her family, their lives their joys and their sorrows would forever remain entwined with her own. She had no time for herself, no secret hopes or desires. She remained a conglomeration of a million other thoughts and faces. There had never been time to build her own dreams, instead she had sighed and smiled and resigned herself to her role as wife and mother.

Now as Devi lay fast asleep next to her mother, Bela looked at her daughter's angular face. Devi had her grandfather's nose and her father's oval eyes. Almond eyes, she thought to herself recalling the first time she had shyly looked into her husband Keshav's thoughtful brown pools. All the rest of her children had inherited her own slightly bulging eyes. She suddenly recalled how Devi had wept on her wedding day. Bela shook herself, not wanting to dwell on the past. The past where Devi was concerned had not been favourable. Sometimes Bela felt regret at forcing Devi into the marriage. There had been tears before and tears that followed. But how was she to know that tragedy would strike so soon after and leave her daughter a grieving widow with young children? As a mother she had thought she was doing her best for her child. Looking at the dark smoothness of her daughter's features, the broadness of her forehead against the dark peak of her hair, Bela's heart felt heavy.

That dreaded phone call on that October morning would always ring loud in her ears, haunting her dreams and her waking hours. That year, death had been an unwelcome visitor within these walls, like a green slime reaching its way upwards across the ceiling and the doors, finding its way into every crevice until the stench was intolerable and the ugly green shouted out to be scrubbed off. It stayed in her bones, leaving the cold clammy ache that was so characteristic of it. It had taken a long time for the sunshine to edge back in, for a giggle to escape through tragedy's unmanned barrier. But was the giggle a momentary lapse of concentration or was tragedy's ominous vigil weakening? The lightening had come with the innocence of the children. Unaware of the prolonged presence of grief, they had let loose joy in their midst until the green and the grey of the walls had reluctantly disappeared to reveal the cowering whites.

She shuddered and shook herself so as not dwell on these thoughts. Devi seemed happier now. Time would slowly heal her wounds. Bela secretly hoped that she had found a man to support her in the lonely years ahead. Now the thought of her grandchildren brought a smile to her face, lighting up her smooth golden skin, the faint wrinkles around her mouth almost flattering her features. She sat up and twisted her serpentine hair into a knot at the nape of her neck. The cool dark of the room with all the shutters closed and the curtains drawn felt as if it was going to close in on her in a moment.

Getting up she pushed open the door of the balcony making sure she would not disturb the sleepers inside. The sun still glared relentlessly down although the world had begun to stir again. The *Kale Jamun* man sat on the porch of the house across the road dangling his feet, throwing an occasional *jamun* into his mouth and spitting out the stones at intervals. The purple juice stained the corners of his mouth, and left dark streaks where he spat. How often Bela had seen him sit there regardless of the afternoon heat; she had wondered where he came from and where he went at the end of the day? Did he have a family and did he earn enough to support them from selling *jamuns* to sleepless people?

She could recall buying *jamuns* from him only once. On another such sleepless afternoon more than a decade ago when Maya and Jai had been asleep indoors and Devi had been happily settled with her husband and children, Bela had waved to the solitary *jamun* seller on the strength of a whim. It had been a long time since she had eaten *jamuns,* usually she waited for her husband to bring some back from the market. That long gone day she had found it hard to resist the call of the *jamun* seller. The man had looked across at the lone figure on the balcony. He had got up, hurriedly lifting his basket of fruit onto his head. He was well tuned to temptation. As the green gates leading to the drive creaked open a younger Bela had slipped lithely downstairs. In the darkness of the kitchen she had rummaged amongst the tins of spices and salt and pepper. One tin held her monthly savings. Clutching at a rupee in her palm she went through the already open front door. She had exchanged a defiant look with her husband who sat on his deck chair in the front porch reading the papers.

"How much are your *jamuns* today, *Dada*?" she had asked the seller as she sat across from the basket on her haunches.

"Eight *anna a pao, Didi,*" he had answered wiping his sweaty forehead with the cloth on which he balanced the basket.

"Let's have a look. They don't look very fresh though, how long have you been carrying them around in the sun?" Bela had eyed the fruit, suspiciously flicking a few over to check their ripeness. She tentatively popped one into her mouth, the sweetness of the purple juices permeated her senses, and she had closed her eyes and let the juices seep out of the corner of her mouth. Her husband had watched, waiting for her to make a decision. It seemed a long time ago that he had seen his wife buying something for herself. He knew Maya and Jai were not yet up from their siesta and she certainly wasn't buying them for him. The summer afternoon was perhaps playing tricks on her mind.

"Give me one *pao*, but don't try and cheat me by putting all the bruised ones in the packet," Bela had said, awaking from her *jamun* reverie.

"No *Didi*, why should I cheat you? Anyway there are no bruised or bad *jamuns*, they are perfect quality, fresh from the orchard, picked by my own hands early this morning," the man had said, taking out his scales and weighing out a few handfuls of the fruit. Bela made sure the scales were perfectly balanced, she didn't want there to be a single fruit less than he owed her. Paying him she had clutched her packet and waited till he had counted out the change,

"What about some salt then?" she had queried knowing how *jamun* sellers could be reluctant to part with the black salt that went so well with the fruit. Out had come the small bag of salt from the recesses of the basket, sprinkling some over the fruit he had waited till she asked him to stop.

As the *jamun* seller walked out of the gate Bela had turned towards her husband now quietly reading. Around her shutters of neighbouring houses were opening, heads hung out to breath in the warm residue of the afternoon. A couple of women had wandered down their *ghats* into the waters of the pond, washing their faces and commencing their evening ablutions. The call of the *jamun* seller could be heard faintly in the distance as he walked into the evening. Bela had offered her husband the packet of fruit,

"Do you want one?" she had asked him. He had shaken his head, still immersed in his paper.

"What about my tea?" he had reminded her as she turned to go.

Bela remembered putting the packet of *jamun* onto the green wooden bench outside the front door meaning to come back to it after she had made his tea. As evening had enveloped the great white house, shutters were closed again to keep out the preying insects. Lights glared on the rectangular balcony, sounds from within the kitchen stirred the night air as mosquitoes hovered over the dusky waters of the pond. There was a quiet lapping of water whilst someone washed dishes in the dark. Bells rang in somebody's *Puja ghar* and conches blew to welcome the dusk.

A seventeen year-old Maya had come out, dressed in her evening best. Her eyes were lined with *kajol* from the earthen lamps making them more predominant in her face. She was going out to meet some friends at the local market place. As she put on her sandals she had noticed the forlorn white paper bag on the green bench. Peering inside she yelped in delight. *Jamuns*! What a treat, Jai must have forgotten about them so they were hers now she had thought with smug delight. She could eat them on her way to the market.

"*Aashchi* Ma," she had called inside as she shut the door, "I'll be back in a couple of hours."

Bela had heard her daughter leave, sitting on her wooden stool next to the burning coals of the earthen stove she prepared dinner for her family. Her face was glowing from the heat, her hands smothered in flour. Perhaps she would get some time to eat her *jamuns* after she had finished in the kitchen. She realised that she had bought them almost four hours ago!

Bela sighed as she thought of how distressed she had been at the end of her tiring evening to find her *jamuns* were no longer there. Her children thought their mother unreasonable over something so trivial. She had refused their offers to buy her more from the market the following day. They hadn't understood the significance of the moment, of the solitary pleasures she had anticipated taking with the luscious fruit in her mouth. It had been an inimitable instant that she had dedicated to herself and yet it had remained unfinished. Her family would always take precedence over her life.

Today, the *jamun* seller looked at her expectantly. Surely he wasn't thinking of that moment they had shared so many years ago. She wasn't even sure whether it was the same man; they all looked the same to her in the blinding light of the afternoon. She turned to go indoors. Devi was awake.

"Ma where were you? Surely it's not time for tea already?"

As Bela lay down again next to her daughter she forgot about salvaging time to herself. She wanted to ask Devi about so many things, to find out about her life in Delhi, which was so much more important to her than her own life here. They chattered on softly into the dregs of the afternoon as the *jamun* seller outside spat one last stone out and walked into the past.

Mother of A Hundred Sons

It had been almost ten years since Sukhi had seen her wedding attire. She looked at it now with a mixture of sorrow and nostalgia. So much had happened to change her life since the day she had worn this sari, so much heartache and pain. She hesitated as she picked the red Banarasi silk out of the battered suitcase, the same case which she had carried with her all those years ago as she came to England for the first time. The matching blouse fell out from within the rustling folds of bright red, letting out whispers of the past; a musty smell of moth balls enveloped her as she gently lifted the material closer to her face, the red and gold silk at once smooth and rough to the touch. A slight tinge of metal came off on her fingers, the tarnish of gold that had long lost its sparkle.

Looking at the sari she thought of the day she had bought it, soon after the decision had been made that she was to marry Raj. She had gone with her mother to the bustling Karol Bagh market in West Delhi to trawl through the endless rows of sari shops. They had stopped at many places, been treated exuberantly and coldly in turn by canny shopkeepers until they had stopped at Bhim Chand and Co., famous for its huge range of wedding *ghagra's* and *choli's*, *sari's* and *lahanga's*. Inside the cool air-conditioned shop mother and daughter had been quite intimidated by the persuasive salesman and his *paan*-chewing spurious enthusiasm.

They knew from his casual familiarity that he did not think them much above his own station. The red juices of *paan* dribbled out of the corner of his mouth, channelling into the creases of his face like a red river dispersing along its shore. He eyed other customers with regret but nevertheless continued to pull out pile after pile of shimmering gold and red and silver and green until Sukhi and her mother could just about see him over the growing mound of silks.

The sari they chose fell out from amongst the pile of vibrant colours. Sukhi had smiled as her mother had pulled the sari towards her approvingly. Momentarily she had felt excited, something that had been absent since her mother had accepted the marriage proposal for her. She remembered now the thrill that the sari had given her as they had packed her suitcase, the excitement and nervousness of being on a plane for the first time, the strangers who surrounded her after she had landed, those who now had become after all these years even stranger than before.

Now as she pulled the sari out of the case, she thought she could see the faint crescent of perspiration under the armpits of her blouse, the salt of her body having stained it forever, marking a point of no return.

Mrs Chawla had been determined to see her daughter married. But when Sukhi turned twenty five she had given up on ever finding the right match for her. Since her husband had died five years ago she had struggled to keep things together at home. Although Sukhi had done her Bachelor's degree she found it hard to find a job. Mrs Chawla herself brought home some money by working in a local nursery school. Delhi was a harsh place to live for a mother and daughter alone and as the days passed Mrs Chawla grew fretful that with their meagre income her daughter would not be eligible for much longer. Letting go of her daughter did mean a lifetime alone for Mrs Chawla, but this was something she did not want to think about yet. After all it would be far worse to have her daughter a spinster.

So when she heard her cousin Shayla talk about her husband's relatives in England who were looking for a girl for their son Raj, Mrs Chawla jumped at the opportunity. She barely consulted her daughter about her choice, informed her that the groom was qualified and worked in the car industry and that the family had requested that the marriage take place in England.

"You will not be alone there *beta*" said Mrs Chawla unconvincingly to Sukhi when she realised that they only had enough money to spare for one ticket.

"Why Manju will come to the wedding and Meena Chachi is like your own mother and besides they are all connected by marriage to us, so it will be like family *na*?"

Sukhi remained silent as her mother went on justifying the reasons why she should make the journey on her own to England, to a distant land to meet an unfamiliar man to whom she would be bound forever. She knew that it was enough that her mother on her meagre school teacher salary was able to afford a one way ticket for her daughter. She did not have the heart to argue with her. And so it was that Sukhi had said farewell to her stoic but inwardly heartbroken mother and made her way to England with a suitcase that held her red and gold wedding sari and a handful of memories of a place she had once called home.

The crowds at Heathrow airport had astounded her as she had pushed her trolley through immigration. She had imagined England to be a quiet place, where people spoke softly and politely and no one shoved and pushed to get ahead. In front of her children ran to hug familiar figures who had been missed; elderly parents were wheeled out by airport staff towards their expectant families, and students shuffled out aimlessly into the cold grey light. There had been no one to greet Sukhi. She found a quiet place next to a blue and white pillar in the arrivals lounge and stood there waiting patiently. Her fair face looked tired and crumpled; her eyes with faint blue circles under them from the tears she had shed on parting from her mother and then the lack of sleep on the flight. She was a pleasant-looking girl at most times, with large brown eyes and very bold eyebrows that met in the middle of her forehead like a sleeping serpent. She was quite tall and her limbs, like most Punjabi girls, were long and athletic. Her usually engaging smile was now missing from her weary face. Instead her cheeks looked creased and sagging, and she appeared far older than her twenty five years.

She had seen a photo of Meena Chachi who was to come and receive her but looking through the crowds she saw nobody who could have looked familiar. Her lips felt parched and her stomach rumbled queerly without associating itself with the familiar pangs of hunger. After forty five minutes, a very round-faced Meena Chachi had appeared with a group of four or five girls of varying ages. She looked at Sukhi in irritation whilst the girls behind her sized her up. They giggled rudely as they stared at her bedraggled *salwaar* suit and her dishevelled hair.

"Sukhi, is it?" said Meena Chachi, a woman of forty plus years who was by now regretting getting involved in this long distance match-making.

"I am sure your mother mentioned that you were fairer than you look, and I expected you to look happier with a name like that?" She clicked her tongue disapprovingly as Sukhi hung her head, unsure of what to say, her name did mean 'happiness' and 'contentment' after all.

"Anyway, too late, eh, word has been given, the boys side will just have to accept you the way you are. Perhaps some make-up will help!" With that she had turned around whilst Sukhi followed, struggling with her suitcase to the car park and then to the place that was to be her home for the next ten days until she was married.

Meena Chachi kept her word and did plaster Sukhi with make-up on her wedding day. Sukhi had by now learnt to accept her brusque manner and sharp words, after all she was the only person vaguely related to her here. The wedding was held in the local community hall. After the ceremony and the *phera's* during which time Sukhi had barely glanced up at her husband's face, she was escorted with her husband to a raised dais where there were two almost throne-like gilt edged chairs. When the wedding reception guests began to arrive, Sukhi barely knew anyone. She had sat gingerly on the edge of her seat as Raj had introduced her to various members of his family. He was a large man, with a thick neck that bulged through the collar of his gold-embroidered *sherwani*, his stomach struggled against the buttons, threatening to pop if he ate or drank anymore throughout the day. Sukhi noticed a small tumbler of whiskey tucked behind his chair which he occasionally sipped at between greeting guests.

Now as she looked down at the sari which she had pulled out after all these years, she remembered her own bashfulness that day, the weight of her sari, the jewels around her neck and the creases of make-up on her face and arms. Later that night she had let her new husband fumble with the clasps on the front of her blouse as she stared fearfully into his red alcohol-puffed face, her husband who she had been told had a right to her body, even though she barely knew him.

That had been ten years ago, now Sukhi shook open the sari, her lips pursed, the first semblance of a tear gently cursing down her cheek.

In ten years Sukhi had not once been back home to her mother in Delhi. She had written to her mother every month, reassured her about how happy she was.

'Raj is a very busy man,' she wrote, 'but he always finds time for the home and for the family.'

By family she meant his mother who lived with them. Although she was old and frail she took it upon herself to be constantly vigilant of her son's young wife. During the day she made sure Sukhi cooked and cleaned and did all that was required of a dutiful daughter-in-law. Nevertheless, whilst Sukhi worked hard at keeping the household in order she was criticised for her cooking, her poor sense of dress and quite often her upbringing. Her mother-in-law took pleasure in reminding her of the meagre dowry she had brought along with her and how she should be eternally grateful for having been married into this household.

Each night Sukhi knew Raj's mother wandered across the hallway to listen at their bedroom door, she heard the slither and hush of her footsteps as she slunk away in the middle of the night. In a strange way she found it reassuring that she was on the other side of the door, waiting to hear their every move, to be party to any secrets they shared. She must have been very disappointed as Raj barely spoke to Sukhi. Behind the closed doors there were no whispers or secrets or endearments. His only interaction with her was physical.

Within a year of her marriage Sukhi was pregnant. There was a sudden change in her mother-in-law's mood during her pregnancy. Now at every opportunity she plied her with food that she felt would make the baby healthy. Bowls of *ghee* that Sukhi was asked to drink; buttered *paratha's* made by her own hands, and all the meat and fruit she desired. Raj, in his rather peremptory way was also quite attentive. Until now she had been barely noticed, but suddenly Sukhi felt spoilt and pampered and wrote glowing letters full of happiness and warmth to her mother. She wrote with plans to visit her once the baby was born. One evening, whilst Raj enjoyed his regular evening whiskey and kebabs, Sukhi even broached the question of a visit. He looked up at her strangely. A sneer crossed his coarse unshaven features. He turned his red eyes round in their bulbous sockets and slurred,

"Once our son is born you are not taking him anywhere. Anyway, why you want to go back to that dump where you lived I don't know. Tell your mother to visit us if you want?"

Sukhi was shocked and taken aback by his words. He had always scorned her coming from India. She knew that he had grown up here having only visited India once when he was twelve. He had come back with nothing else but a severe case of dysentery. Although his parents had raised him to follow Indian customs he was like many of his generation dispassionate about the country itself. She knew he had been forced to marry her; that his mother had requested that he marry a girl from India as they were known to be compliant and good housewives. That was all that had recommended her to him. It suddenly occurred to Sukhi that he did not know the sex of the child.

"How do you know that it is a boy?" she asked him abruptly just as her mother-in-law shuffled in with another plate of steaming hot kebabs. Mother and son exchanged questioning looks. Now Raj's mother went up to her daughter-in-law and pinched her cheek in a mock gesture of affection. Sukhi felt the coarseness of her thumb and forefinger on her cheek, her skin near hers glowing from the heat of the kitchen, her old wrinkled face painstakingly distorted into a mock smile.

"*Arre, Beti*," she said to Sukhi "Think good thoughts. If God wants then you will be blessed with a hundred sons. Look at me and my two sons. I am truly blessed *na*? Don't make your mind negative, okay, here have a kebab." And just like that Sukhi felt scared for the child moving stealthily inside her belly, innocently waiting to be born.

The baby was a girl. That day the entire family looked upon her with contempt. As he stood next to her hospital bed Raj had sworn at Sukhi, in Punjabi, so that the English nurse would not understand what he was saying. His crude and unkind words struck fear in Sukhi's heart. Her mother-in-law had clicked her tongue and pursed her lips as she stood there. She said nothing, did not offer to hold the baby or ask after the mother. She shuffled away angrily with her son at her side. Later, when they had left, Sukhi lay alone in the hospital bed with her daughter in her arms and shed tears for the infant, knowing that she was unwelcome, knowing that like herself she was to be a stranger forever to the household.

Her mother-in-law's gestures of kindness at home ceased abruptly. She would even put a lock on the fridge daring Sukhi to eat more than she was offered at dinner or lunch. As the baby suckled at her breast, Sukhi often felt faint with hunger and exhaustion. Even before her wounds from child birth had healed Raj had lurched into the bedroom drunk and angry one night, cursed her for giving birth to a female child and thereby humiliating him in society. He had his way with Sukhi until she cried with agony. Nine months later she gave birth to their second daughter, this time there was less fuss made over her beforehand and afterwards she was once again with her two children spurned.

As the girls grew up, Sukhi mutely continued in her role as the perfect wife. Raj would now find it tempting to hit her when he was angry or drunk and she lived in constant fear of his presence. In her letters to her mother she continued to write that all was well, telling her about her two beautiful granddaughters, Simona and Shirin, and hoping that they would be able to meet one day soon.

In September of Sukhi's fifth year away, Mrs Chawla met with an accident. It was all very sudden. On her way to the post office her rickshaw was pulled underneath the wheels of an errant DTC bus. It was all very quick, both the rickshaw puller and Mrs Chawla died instantly. In Mrs Chawla's handbag was a letter she had written to Sukhi telling her that she had saved enough money to visit her during the following spring break. Her relatives in India sent Sukhi the letter hoping it would help her as she mourned her parent.

For Sukhi it seemed that her entire past was severed with the death of her mother. She had taken with her any ties of the life she had lived before. Relative to her existence now, those had been simpler more carefree days. When she had left her mother in Delhi she had not thought as she had waved goodbye that she would never see her again.

The only place Sukhi could find solace was in the company of her two young daughters. She stayed in her room for three days and even Raj kept his distance from her during this time. After this Sukhi came out knowing that she was needed for her daughters, swearing to herself that she would not part with them for as long as she could. She would find a way somehow to keep hold of them, to let them make their own choices in the world. She thought of the long years ahead of her, Raj's beatings, his mother's sharp tongue and her courage almost failed her. Looking into the eyes of her daughters she vowed that things would change.

Life resumed. After the tragedy each day slowly and painfully distanced itself from the past until memories of her mother remained a weak shadow of her life now. As her daughters started at the local school Sukhi found it liberating to be out doors. Dropping them off and picking them up however briefly each day was enough to escape the constant menace of her mother-in-law and the drudgery of her work load.

She had a third child, another daughter as beautiful as the sunshine on a cold winter's day. Now Sukhi no longer cried when her children were born, instead she immersed herself in the care of her new-born and disregarded all else around her. The sarcastic relatives, the increasingly aggressive husband and the acrid mother-in-law; she seemed to close down the shutters of her mind to them.

The beatings slowly became worse. Sukhi learnt not to cry or scream when he was in one of his drunken rages, she just carried on as before picking herself up from the floor and camouflaging her bruises as well as possible the following day. Sometimes at night she would lie down next to her daughters asleep in their beds. When the moon shone through the curtains on their innocent faces she wept quiet tears, alone and helpless, yearning for the past in Delhi when things were so uncomplicated.

One autumn afternoon as she stood waiting for her daughters in the school playground Sukhi saw Mr Bramley the school headmaster approach her. At first she was anxious. Had someone noticed her recent bruises and informed him, or perhaps her daughters had mentioned something at school? After all the girls knew what went on behind the closed doors of their parents' room; they sensed their father's growing distaste for their mother and his hostility towards all of them. The eldest, nine-year old Shirin, had once come quietly forward to help her mother put ice on her arm where the bruise was quickly turning from red to an ugly green. Sukhi had tried to smile but one look into her daughter's serious eyes she knew that it was too late to make up a story about her injury, she could see the hurt of knowledge behind the mist of the child's sad eyes.

"Mrs Bhatia," said the smiling headmaster as he approached her, "I wonder if you would like to take part in a new scheme we are starting here?" he waited expecting curiosity from Sukhi but she stood quietly her eyes darting over his shoulders to see her daughters so that she could find an excuse to escape.

"We have decided to initiate a small class for some of the mother's who would like to improve their English." he continued warmly and expectantly to Sukhi.

It took Sukhi a few seconds to comprehend what he was saying and she then shook her head warily, knowing that she would not be allowed to stay out of the house for longer than she should.

"It is something that will fit in with the school run in the afternoon" he said encouragingly, knowing why she looked so wary and unsure. He had seen that look before, the temptation guarded by the weight of the responsibilities many of the women were forced to take at home.

"A student from the local university is going to be here every Wednesday afternoon to talk to ladies from the subcontinent and discuss their language and social needs. It's a new scheme so we thought if you and a few other ladies were interested it could take off?" He waited for her response but she shook her head, unsure, her life was already so complicated, she didn't need much more.

"You will be part of your daughter's school?" he said persuasively, knowing that most mother's would be curious to actually be inside the school during the working day. Sukhi found herself accepting to come for the class the following Wednesday. Just this once, she thought to herself unconvincingly.

On Wednesday Sukhi lied to her mother-in-law, saying she had to attend to something for her daughters at the school. Before she left, pushing her youngest in the pram along the damp autumn roads, Sukhi felt unsure about what she was doing. In all these years she had never had the opportunity to do anything for herself. Her life had been a flurry of babies and cooking and beatings and disappointments. She realised that she had become the least important person in her own life. The cold air crept through her nylon *salwar kameez*, the legs billowing beneath her black coat, a cut on her exposed upper lip felt raw in the cold wind. As she reached the school gates she saw a few other women approaching with trepidation in their footsteps, just like herself. They nodded to each other, unsure, awkward at being there at such an odd time without the children bustling around them, craving their attention. They felt naked and exposed without their usual appendages. Now they acknowledged each other without saying much, just a few nodding heads in the afternoon sun.

The headmaster met them warmly at the door and led them into a small empty classroom. There was a quiet hum of activity in the school which comforted Sukhi. The knowledge that her daughters were safe here away from the festering tensions of their home reassured her. She settled her youngest, now asleep in the pram, in a corner of the room whilst they sat awkwardly around a low table on small red plastic chairs, awaiting the teacher. They did not know what to expect, or for that matter how to behave once the teacher was here. They knew they would not be able to come regularly, ensnared as they were in the rigours of their lives at home.

The door opened and the headmaster came in smiling at the women. Behind him was a young girl of about twenty, looking nervous and unsure.

"This is Tara Sen," he said by way of introduction. "She will be taking this session with you ladies and I hope it will be immensely beneficial" he said with enthusiasm. He looked at the teacher momentarily hesitating, almost taken aback himself at the youthfulness of her appearance.

"If there is anything you need Miss Sen, please do not hesitate to ask me. My office is just around the corner. And of course provisions have been made for all of you ladies for tea and coffee. So please help yourselves." He pointed towards a shelf with a kettle and some cups on it, and then smiling nervously he left the room.

There was an awkward silence as the motley group of students and youthful teacher observed each other.

"*Namastey,*" said Tara Sen in greeting, she smiled and her dimpled cheeks added to her youthfulness.

"It's so nice to meet people from home, I miss it so much." she said and with those few words Tara Sen immediately befriended herself to that roomful of lonely women.

At the end of the class Sukhi found herself walking outside with the young teacher as she headed towards the playground where her daughters were waiting. They began talking, Sukhi at first shy and reluctant but encouraged by Tara's amiability.

Tara came from the same suburb of West Delhi where Sukhi had grown up. When she discovered this Sukhi enquired hungrily about the places she knew. They spoke excitedly about their common haunts and Sukhi who had left it all behind so long ago listened with a sense of nostalgia about how things had changed since or perhaps remained unchanged. She asked her about the market in Karol Bagh, the famous *chaat* shops in Patel Nagar and the cinema hall just across the road from them. She smiled when she heard about the overpass that had been made to help the masses and how it was only used by the stray dogs of the neighbourhood, the stench of their faeces wafting down to the road below. Tara told her how the College for errant boys on the corner of Rajni Nagar had been removed, and Sukhi thrilled at this when she remembered how she had been scared to pass by on her own way back home from College.

On Wednesdays now Sukhi woke up with a great sense of excitement. She hurried through her morning chores and then found excuses each week to make it early to the school to attend Tara's class. They greeted each other like old friends and although Tara continued with a small curriculum of English for the entire group to follow, it was soon obvious that this was an excuse for the two of them to meet.

When Sukhi learnt that Tara lived in a shared student house and cooked her own meals she started bringing her secret goodies. Parathas wrapped in foil, mutton kebabs from the previous evenings dinner or a bowl of mixed vegetables. Tara relished these home-cooked items. Her young face dimpled with delight when Sukhi snuck a small bag in her hands at the end of a lesson. She wished she could do something in return for her. Sukhi never told Tara that she had to come to the class secretly, she never mentioned her unhappiness at home, the beatings from her husband, but as their friendship grew Tara sensed the older woman's unhappiness.

For Sukhi just being in the company of this young liberated girl was enough to make her forget the pain of her own wretched existence. In Tara, Sukhi saw her own self, the self that never had a chance to survive in the different circumstances that her own life had been overwhelmed by. Tara's sense of freedom was her own, her life as a young single woman in a foreign country was the life she could have chosen if only she had the choice. Now all she wished for was that her own daughters could follow Tara's path in their lives. She hoped they could break free from the shackles of tradition and embrace the modern with open arms. For herself she knew it was too late but for the present she savoured her moments away from home in the small class in that local primary school.

Just before Easter, Raj lost his job. The motor vehicle industry in Coventry was tiring out, the days of luxury car making were dwindling and slowly the work force was cut down to the bare minimum. Where machines could do the job of ten, the machines indeed took over and the men were sent home. Raj sat around sullenly at home. His drinking habits got worse, but these days nothing bothered Sukhi as much as it had done in the years before.

Recently, Tara had got the ladies to contribute recipes to a little book which she was going to print out with the headmaster's permission and this caused a lot of excitement amongst them. Tara had asked Sukhi to take on the responsibility of putting the recipes in order. So each night Sukhi took out the folder of pages from beneath her daughter's bed where she had hidden it and pored over each one to see how they could best be put together. She could hear her husband snoring noisily next door, her daughters' hushed breathing above her. Under the light of a bed lamp she hugged the folder close to her chest, happier than she had been in a long time. Her own contribution was a recipe of her mothers: a light gravy of cottage cheese and peas which Sukhi had loved to eat in the winter months in Delhi. She looked at the sheet where she had painstakingly written the recipe out with Tara's help. She thought of her mother, how they would eat together on a wooden *charpouy* on the roof; the fresh yoghurt which would accompany every meal. Would her mother be happy if she saw her now? Sukhi thought wistfully.

On Wednesday that week when she came home in the afternoon with the girls Raj was not slumped as usual on the sofa. As they approached the house she saw him peering out of the net curtains. He came forward to meet them as they came through into the house. There was an eerie glint in his eyes which Sukhi found disconcerting. Ignoring the girls he asked Sukhi where she had been. At first Sukhi was taken aback, she had been so sure that her secret was safe that she had quite forgotten to be scared of being found out.

"To the school of course," she lied with her head bent down. She busied herself with the girls' jackets and shoes, giving them a snack and glasses of milk. She felt Raj's eyes following her around the room, a slow nasty grin stretching across his alcohol-puffed features. Her mother-in-law sat watching television, her jaws set smugly in a satisfied severity.

As Sukhi bent down to put the girls' shoes away in the cupboard in the front hall she heard his footsteps follow her. The kick in her side winded her momentarily and she fell forward, her forehead hitting the corner of the shoe rack. At first she felt no pain, just the desperation to catch her breath as it left her lungs and whooshed out of her open mouth. The next kick was more painful, a searing pain shot through to her neck from her stomach, sharp and fiery.

"You whore," he shouted. "Do you think I don't know what you have been up to? Think I am a fool? Cavorting with people outside the home, you fucking liar."

Sukhi heard his shouts and screams from a distant place; her mind was still accommodating itself to the physical shock. She heard the patter of her daughters feet, their screams as they saw their mother on the floor the blood dribbling down her forehead past her ears in angry rivulets. They tried to get past their father but he pushed them back into the room and shut the door as he continued to shout and kick their mother. It seemed like hell for Sukhi, a bottomless hole from where there was no escape. She tried to crawl away upstairs but he pulled her down, and thrashed her until the fabric of her *salwar kameez* tore against her back exposing her skin. Somehow this enraged him even more and he rained down blows relentlessly. What seemed like hours later the girls came and pulled their mother upstairs, their terrified tear-stricken faces more painful for Sukhi than all the abuse and hurt she had just been through.

In the days which followed, Raj started taking the girls to school and back. Sukhi stayed at home, soundless and resigned. The grief she felt inside her was more than she remembered when her mother had died. That afternoon when she dragged out her old suitcase she decided that she needed to find her own way out. Looking down upon the sari that had come so far with her, she knew that she was hopelessly bound to her current state. She thought of Tara, and hoped there would be someone like her to guide her daughters. As she wrapped the sari around her neck she cried for her daughters, wishing that she could be around to help them escape too, but perhaps her going would be a sign to them, a sign that they must find their own ways out of here.

She poured the spirit over the sari, its sharp heady odour making her feel light- headed. Her tears fell soundlessly on the red material and her tongue felt thick as the blood pounded through her body. Her heart seemed to be swelling and throbbing inside her like an enormous painful growth. Her blood hammered and pounded in her ears. She shut her eyes as she lit a match and ignited the past.

The Odd Couple

When I first arrived in England, I remember only the searing pain in both my arms. This was from the weight of the mangoes my mother had judiciously packed as gifts for her friends. In my left hand was the guilty yellow straw bag, preserved from a distant trip to the mountains, the handles of which were so thick and coarse that they chafed the skin of my palms.

Back in Kolkata airport I had barely handled my baggage. A resourceful neighbour whom we addressed as 'Choto Kaku' or 'Youngest Uncle' had driven us to the airport. Having spent his entire life in the same city, Choto Kaku nurtured even the slightest of acquaintances, in the hope of a friendly barter of favours at any point in his life. Over the years he had cultivated friends and allies at the airport where he had driven on numerous occasions to drop off friends and relatives. The airport teemed with unknown people, travelling, working, begging for money, yet invariably when in Choto Kaku's company, there would suddenly appear a friendly face, saying pleasantly, "How are you Shoumen?" Or, "Hey Shoumen Da where have you been all this time?" and then a conversation would follow, at once polite and unceremonious, until Shoumen, or Choto

Kaku as I knew him, would clasp his acquaintances hand in both of his and wink and smile and ask that he be allowed to escort his ward further into the inner depths of the airport. In my case, his acquaintance, in exchange for a bottle of whiskey from the duty free shop, had allowed Choto Kaku right up to the aircraft itself. Once inside I also realised, much to my discomfort at the time that I had been upgraded to first class.

I must admit that it was a wasted use of the first class. The lushness, the curtained-off privacy, the fresh-smelling business executives returning home to their families after their interesting trips to India; suitcases neatly packed with expensive *kantha* silks and pashmina shawls; statues of Ganesh and Laxmi in brass and marble, wrapped and snuggled into the depths of their luggage. Later, these tokens of their visit would be central to many a dinner party conversation; about how intriguing India was as a country but "Oh so filthy" and how badly his stomach had suffered from the food and water and how the teeming poor would not leave him alone. These executives would sit in their perfectly-designed homes, whilst their relics of the journey nestled in the shadows of a winter evening and shed invisible tears.

It had been a while since I had boarded an aeroplane. The last time was when my mother and I had returned home, alone without my father. His ashes remained in a numbered plot in a Surrey cemetery, the unknown Indian man, who had travelled afar to build his future and left his life behind instead. Huddled into a tin canister we had flown across the skies, my mother's tears thwarted by my constant air sickness.

I recalled how the plane had developed engine trouble mid-air, coughing and spluttering it had made an emergency landing at Kabul airport. The landscape became one of my most haunting childhood memories, mountainous and unfriendly, enveloping the heat and dust of the airport tarmac. Rifle-toting guards stood around us, their eyes beady and unmoving, their sweat-encrusted *salwar* tunics damp and uncompromising. After fourteen hours of being confined in the airport lounge we had re-boarded our flight, found our way back to our vomit reeking seats and held on for dear life until the plane had landed in Kolkata. It was almost as if we had been catapulted across the seas in a messy and awkward sling shot. That was the last time I had flown. Now, almost twenty years later, at a little changed international airport I was heading back to where it had all begun.

My nerves were on edge, as the plane soared into the sky and left behind the lonely twinkling lights of the city in which I had grown up and yet now found it so easy to abandon. I thought I saw my mother wave from amongst the green and drooping coconut palms. A sad wave that only mothers can do when a daughter leaves home, be it on her wedding day or when she leaves for a foreign land.

As the plane soared towards the moon, I shed a few solitary tears much to the discomfort of my fellow passenger, a sharp, well-travelled businessman. I am sure he had been hoping for a more companionable executive, but here he was with this young Bengali woman, trepidation in the air, a resigned irritation as he tried not to look as the soundless tears rolled down my cheeks.

Perhaps that flight like so many others from Kolkata, with so many more aspiring people like me, took off and a myriad of silent tears were shed like raindrops that fell glittering to the warm earth of Bengal to feed its luminous vegetation. That is perhaps the secret to Bengal's lushness, the tears it collects when flights take off with so many hopefuls, like a sad bunch of migratory birds.

*

The road that led away from the three bedroom terraced house was pleasant enough. Leading down the hill at one end and up towards the famous Epsom Downs at the other, it smiled in a lopsided, quirky kind of way to anyone who looked upon it from a distance.

As I peered through the creamy white net curtains of my window I was often overwhelmed by loneliness, by the consequences of my decision to leave everything behind and come and stay on this lonesome smirking stretch of road. I looked upon a row of terraced houses with their closed fronts and immaculate gardens, faceless homes where I rarely saw anybody come out. Sometimes I would see a dog run along the pavement; and then wait impatiently for its owner at the corner that led up onto the Downs. At those moments I would smile at my window and feel a sense of harmony with my surroundings and I never failed to appreciate that after all these years living amidst the clamour of Kolkata, I had finally managed to find a place to think.

Cecilia and Martin Gail lived by themselves with their pet cat, Snowball; a puffed up arrogant creature fed on Cecilia's homely cooking, who I occasionally found asleep on my pillow in what it obviously used to know as its own room. I came to stay soon after my mother wrote to request her friends that they could take me in as their guest until the start of Michaelmas at Oxford. They had welcomed me kindly; their letters to my mother over the years had been full of nothing but warmth and sincerity even though they managed to maintain a semblance of their English reserve.

I had come to England without an immediate plan. The summer stretched ahead of me and I knew my stay here was temporary, a stop-gap before I went my own way. This was the place where I had spent the first five years of my childhood and over the years growing up in Kolkata the memories had never quite faded. With each letter that my mother received from her friends in England I clamoured to hear their news, to acknowledge that the part of our lives which had been cut short so suddenly had not been completely obliterated. Whilst we adjusted with difficulty to our lives in Kolkata, life here on this street, on a quiet hillside had continued as before. When I looked around myself nothing had really changed except me. There was the alley where I had fallen down on my way to the shops with my mother, rugged and secret with the constant odour of overripe pears. The pear tree I remembered still hung over it, the fruit which I had once coveted as a child rotting in brown grainy puddles of mush.

The houses down the road stood the same, just the inhabitants had moved or grown up and left, trees and shrubs remained where I had left them. The Gail's house had the same gnarled outside walls, white and mottled with time, the front door a deep shade of blue. Even the carpets and wallpaper in the living room were unchanged. I noted a scribble on the corner of a wall leading to the garden; was this where their daughter Sarah and I had giggled together one summer afternoon and scrawled our names with an illicit crayon? Later we were caught and reprimanded, just like we had been for plucking the buds off the rose bushes one afternoon and leaving the garden bare. Cecilia had been distraught, but Martin had managed to placate her and I had left for my home that evening feeling remorseful and guilty. When I had met Sarah the following evening we played quietly in the road at the front, steering clear of the garden. Strange, how my misdemeanours came to mind first, before any other pleasanter memories. Nevertheless I remembered that summer, vividly, more so for the reason that it would be our last there.

I had the smallest space in the house. A miniscule square which had a high single bed and a dresser, after which there was barely enough room to move around. My suitcase Martin very kindly kept in the guest room at the back, a larger room piled high with all kinds of rejected furniture and a huge double bed in the middle. I was not offered this room.

Yet, I learnt to love my small box room. It was bright and cosy and I had a little radio and a stack of books over my head which I was free to use. The radio tuned only to a single pop station blared out the latest tunes accompanied by a cheerful friendly commentary. I arranged my solitary pink lipstick and cream pot on top of the dresser where there was a smiling picture of a young Cecilia in fresh white tennis gear on a lovely summer's day looking straight into the future.

They had lived in this house for over thirty years now. It had been inherited from Martin's mother and they had moved here soon after they had been married. It was in this house that they had their four children; celebrated their numerous birthdays, wept at their troubles and shortcomings and finally sighed with mixed regret and relief when they had left home. And it was down this road that they had first met my parents when they had arrived in this country and moved into the yellow house behind the chestnut tree at the corner of the street.

Coming back to this house, after so many years, I found fleeting memories of high teas, celery standing erect in glasses, jam and Marmite sandwiches, luscious scented strawberries and the hush of an English summer gently floating through the open French windows at the back. Sometimes as I stood and looked out into the street in front, I felt as though I had never left, never flown back with a heart-broken mother to the land where she felt we belonged, with memories of a lost childhood which I had carried begrudgingly all these years.

Now, in the smallness of my room, I felt a strange sense of belonging to something which however briefly had been part of my life. But as well as this, I realised that what gave me most pleasure was the joy of having a space of my own. I revelled in the thought that if I desired I could stand on my head, cut my toenails, sing, dance or just do nothing at all, in the company of only myself. It was in this room that I planned the future, sat cross-legged on my bed and thought of the luminous spires of Oxford where I was headed. It was here in this miniscule space that I vowed never to return to the life I had led so far. This cramped room, with its oversized furniture became the head quarters of a life that aspired to be ordinary and nothing less than that.

Cecilia was suspicious of Mangoes. I could see her look worried as I unpacked the now overripe fruit onto her spotless kitchen work-top. My mother had packed the mangoes carefully into the yellow bag. She had wrapped them with some of my clothes to protect them from bruising, so now I had vests, t-shirts and a skirt which smelt strongly of mango and the musty straw which still stuck to their sticky oozing skin. Perhaps it was this sickly sweet aroma of mango and straw on my clothes which so enamoured Martin, perhaps it added to the exotic air that I unknowingly brought to their three bedroom terraced house that summer and changed their lives forever. I would never know, perhaps it was the mangoes.

I showed them how to cut the yellow slippery fruit; I had never ever attempted to do so before myself. Back home it was always cut and placed before me in a bowl to enjoy. Now as I stood over the kitchen sink, the fruit squelching and slipping around in my yellow-stained fingers, I bravely sliced through the sides whilst leaving the centre intact. I then demonstrated to Cecilia and Martin how to peel and suck the stone, remove the rind and scoop out the fruit from the bowl-shaped outer parts. They watched me, Cecilia warily and Martin at first aghast and then with a sudden forced burst of enthusiasm and politeness so quintessential of the English. He lifted up a sliver to his mouth and ate noisily and gustily in a poor attempt to imitate me. I was relieved at first to see how he shared my enthusiasm, but as I watched the juices of the fruit dribble down his pale hairless chin I felt a creeping sense of repulsion and disdain. I would have preferred it if like his wife he had shown a reluctance to try the fruit, instead his almost forced actions felt gauche and ugly and left me feeling uncomfortable. I was glad when Cecelia suggested politely that I put the mangoes away in the fridge so that they could enjoy them at a later time. I knew the sight of her husband secretly annoyed and disgusted her as well.

The mangoes rotted in the fridge, their skin grew mottled and brown over the next few days and every time the fridge was opened a pungent smell enveloped the small house. I dared not mention them to Cecilia again and neither did she, until one day I opened the fridge to see they were gone and a fresh sharp smell of cleaning fluid replaced the sickly sweet odour of the fruit.

I needed to find myself a job until I went up to Oxford. I was determined to pay Cecilia and Martin some rent although they were very kind and told me not to worry. Cecilia worked as a secretary in a law firm. She was due to retire the following year after nearly twenty five years of service in the same company. In the mornings I would come down to find she had left for work and Martin, who was already retired, would be doing the breakfast dishes in the kitchen, singing along to music on the kitchen radio, rubber gloves on and a flowered apron over his day clothes. He was a handsome old man, with thin silver hair and a young boyish face. It occurred to me how little his face had changed from before, except for a few lines near his eyes, he had not really aged and I knew he was nearly seventy by then. He had a lovely warm smile and his voice was young and cheery when he greeted me in the morning.

"How did you sleep?" he would ask, rubber gloves dripping suds over the kitchen floor.

"I do hope your room is comfortable. I do apologise for it being so small." He meant this sincerely and expressed regret almost every day for it, little did he know how much that space had begun to mean to me. How different it was from the home I had left back in India.

Whilst I had breakfast, Martin would sit next to me and we would talk about the day ahead of us. Now that he was retired he looked after the house and did all the chores. He did the laundry and the ironing and then the garden and occasionally whizzed out in the car to get the groceries which Cecilia had listed out for him. At first I was reluctant to join him for anything. I found his eagerness and helpfulness slightly disconcerting. Male members of the family in India had always been gruff and peremptory, finding little in common with me. Living alone with my mother had made me awkward with visiting male relatives as well. They were creatures whom we stayed away from, left to watch TV or read the papers. They were fed before any of us, alone at the table whilst mothers and aunts hovered over them seeing to their needs.

At first chary of Martin I got used to his ways. When he saw me writing out job applications by hand he showed me how to use his electronic typewriter and we would both sit together and plan out my next letter. He guided me as best he could until like co-conspirators we would feel satisfied with the results. One morning he took me to a local employment agency, armed with my CV and a huge ego. At the agency Martin sat quietly next to me, smiling as if I was his own prodigy. The agent looked through my CV slowly, the youthfulness of my looks leaving him unconvinced about my qualifications.

In the afternoons Martin and I would sit down to lunch in front of the TV. Cecilia made a plate of salad for each of us before she left for work. There would be a portion of potato salad, coleslaw, some tomatoes and cucumbers and a piece of tinned fish. She would leave both plates wrapped in cling film inside the fridge ready for us. At noon Martin would draw up the chairs in the living room towards the television set and we would sit together like an old couple with our plates on our knees watching the latest episode of 'Neighbours'. Back home we had not owned a television set. When we had returned to India, our lives were dry and sparing, not just from the lack of a TV but from most other joyous things that other families took for granted, like dinners together around a dining table or holidays or visitors in the evening.

Soon after I started at university, my mother would occasionally venture out into the world with me and I would take her shopping at *Dakhinapan* where we picked up cotton printed night dresses for her from the colourful stalls outside or a piece of material from *Gurjari* for myself. Later we would go to *Krystal Chopsticks* in Triangular Park where we carefully ordered from the menu. Unfamiliar with eating out we were reserved and frugal but those were relatively happy evenings.

On Sunday mornings I would go to a neighbour's house and sit on a metallic chair near their door to watch Star Trek. I loved those mornings, Captain Kirk visiting unknown lands confronting unknown dangers, always managing to come out the hero. In the afternoon I would walk back my head full of dreams to lunch at my desk alone in our room whilst my mother finished the housework.

Now sitting with Martin for lunch in front of the television was a treat. I soon got used to the colourful lives of the Neighbours from Australia; we began to share a common interest in something foreign, not just each other. When the recruitment agent called with an interview at a local firm, I whooped with joy and hugged Martin. Momentarily we danced around the living room, Martin clumsily tripping over the fluffy mat, the furniture knocked around as a surprised Snowball fled from her perch on a chair. We giggled together whilst we finished the rest of our lunch and later that afternoon Martin took me for a drive along the stunning Epsom Downs.

In the evening when Cecilia came home from work she found us both in the kitchen, the radio on full blast whilst I made a mess trying to teach Martin how to cook potato fritters. I was completely out of my depth in the kitchen. The fritters were half cooked, and crunchy, the batter damp and greasy. I heard Cecilia reprimand a sheepish Martin for encouraging a mess. She was tired and needed to cook dinner and this was not a 'funhouse'. Later, over a magnificent shepherds pie and peas I told Cecilia about my interview the following day. She was happy for me, her round face was kind and open and her frizz of golden hair shone like a halo around her. She looked older than Martin though, and tired. Somehow I began to scorn her. I was suddenly so conscious of my youth, my shining skin, and long dark hair. By then I knew Martin was mesmerised by it all, by my heavy accent, my perfect English diction, my confidence for the future. With the offer of the interview my confidence had surged and I felt that a full and wholesome life lay before me. Their small house seemed suddenly even smaller, barely able to contain my visions for the future. At night I lay restless in bed, imagining the interview, when I would, no doubt, shine forth as a rising star.

In the morning after breakfast, a freshly showered and shaved Martin drove me to the offices. He came in with me to the reception desk and sat and waited as an amused English receptionist took me inside. There were two people who waited to interview me. A sharp-faced blonde lady in her mid-forties, who smiled with thin pursed lips as I walked in, and a square-jawed man in a dark blue suit who seemed quite a bit older than her. I sat down in a chair set on the opposite side of a large desk behind which they both sat. They began by asking me a few questions about when I had arrived in England and how my experience had been so far.

"So how do you see yourself in the future?" the lady asked me. Her voice was firm, refined, slightly tinged with arrogance.

"Well" I began coughing slightly to clear my throat, "I begin my research degree at Oxford in September. I shall work until then and leave."

I said this with a slight upward tilt of my chin, believing that mention of Oxford should be enough to impress them. Also, I had been told how much the English loved truthfulness, honesty being the best policy in anything. I saw their expressions change from interest to intrigue.

"So you are planning to quit just before term starts?" he asked me gravely, his brows knitting together. They looked at each other quizzically, unsure, then he nodded at her and turned to me, handing me back my resume.

"I'm afraid there has been some kind of misunderstanding. We were actually looking for somebody who would be committed on a permanent basis. It is the recruitment agent's fault; he should have clarified it to you."

I took back my folder, not quite sure what he meant. Surely he could not be turning me down. I had been honest, I was so qualified!!

They shook hands with me and the man opened the door to let me out. I felt that I should say something more but he smiled and the door shut firmly behind me. Outside in the waiting room, Martin sat reading a magazine. He looked up and smiled at me hopefully. As we walked outside I told him what had happened. We drove home in a deflated silence.

Once home I went up to my room and lay on my bed and thought of my life. It was my first rejection in England, a land where I had hoped nothing I would do could be turned down. I had received the first harsh blow to the vanity and assuredness of my youth and ignorance. It would be the beginning of many. I heard a knock on my door. A gentle tap and Martin nudged the door open. His kind face smiled at me as he held out a cup of tea. I sat up, crossing my legs, there was no where else to sit so he handed me the cup and stood awkwardly at the door.

"Don't worry dear, you will be fine," he said "You were right in whatever you said. It would have been awkard to leave when you needed to otherwise."

I knew he was right, I knew this was not a slander on my capabilities, yet suddenly for the first time I felt completely lost and alone, small and bewildered. No longer did I feel the confidence with which I had arrived here, instead all the feelings of positive euphoria which had built up over the past few days now slowly ebbed away. As the tears welled up in my eyes Martin hurriedly took back my cup of tea wobbling in my outstretched hand. He put it on the dresser and then sat next to me on the bed. I felt his arm around my shoulders, gentle and soft, the slight smell of Marmite from his shirt left over from his toast in the morning.

I thought of my mother back home; her hopes for me, her reluctance to let me leave and now Martin's kindness and understanding. It was

Martin who had helped take my father to hospital after his stroke, after my mother had run out onto the street knocking on their door asking for help one Sunday afternoon in September when her husband had collapsed on the dining room floor. It was Martin that had called an ambulance and gone with my mother in his car whilst Cecilia took me under her wing, looked after me that evening and into the night until her husband had come home with my mother. We had stayed here that night, both of us huddled in the bed in the guestroom. In the morning Martin had again taken my mother to the hospital whilst Cecilia sent me to school with her own children. It was that afternoon when I was picked up early by my mother that I realised what had happened. My father had died that night; he was thirty five years old, the victim of a heart attack. Later I found out from whispered conversations between my mother and aunts the details of that afternoon, the stone- faced doctors and the stark hospital wards where Martin had held my mother's hand and prayed.

In the days which followed, I remember spending long periods in this house whilst my mother packed up our home. In a week the memories of that house were brushed out with the remnants of my childhood. The day we left for the airport my mother had wept on Cecilia's shoulder. A part of us was left behind on that street, forever, a part of us we would never really forget.

Here I was now, in the same house, twenty years later. Somehow I felt that Martin's gestures of kindness towards me that day were not quite as innocent as I thought. I tried to reassure myself that it was just an exchange of kindness, a need for warmth and understanding, but I knew that in his mind he had crossed some boundaries, that what he felt towards me was not so innocent or generous as before. I felt sick with exhaustion from the events of the day and now suddenly repulsed by Martin's proximity. Downstairs I was relieved to hear

Cecilia come home, her key in the lock. Martin got off my bed guiltily and went downstairs to greet her. I was terrified of going downstairs; the room seemed to close in on me, to accuse me of a crime I had not committed, once again like when I had plucked the rosebuds of the bushes so many summers ago. I sat like stone on my bed, unable to move.

Later I realised that Cecilia had put my absence at dinner down to my disappointment at the interview. Martin told her everything and they enjoyed the living room to themselves once again, with Snowball for company. The following morning I showered and came down after I heard Cecilia leave for work. There he was in his yellow marigolds and flowered apron whistling as he did the dishes. He sounded so happy and unconcerned. As he heard my footsteps he turned around, his face beaming, his smile stretching across it, welcoming the entire world.

"Hello there sleepy head. Do you feel better this morning?" I nodded my head lying, pretending to smile, my face aching my heart a wretched mess.

"Come on then, let's get you some breakfast. You must be starving."

He behaved as if the events of the previous afternoon no longer existed. He smiled and whistled all through the morning and it was only when we sat down to lunch, together in front of an episode of 'Neighbours' that I was again able to enjoy the warmth of the present moment, a togetherness which I had barely anticipated when I walked into their home that morning not so long ago.

I did finally find myself a job that summer, teaching foreign students at the local school. This is where the fact that I would soon be going to Oxford to study English counted, where students from

France and Spain learnt that even if you were not English you could master the language to perfection. I was a good example for them and the summer went by fast. I did pay Cecilia the fifteen pounds a week which I had promised her and she took it gracefully. Martin continued to be enamoured by me. He asked me if I meditated, said he would like to learn Indian spiritualism. He brought back books from the library about Indian art and culture and even suggested to Cecilia one evening that they should watch an Indian movie. It was then I knew that Cecilia began to suspect something. At night I heard them arguing in the next room, their voices hushed, knowing I was able to hear every word they said. Cecilia became a little brusque with me, she asked me often when I was thinking of leaving for Oxford, I knew she hoped I would leave earlier.

One morning after she had left Martin came into my room, he laid his head on my shoulder, and I patted him awkwardly. At work I had two very young and bright co-teachers who absorbed my thoughts more these days. I began to feel awkward at Martin's increased advances, slightly repulsed like the day I saw him eating mangoes in the kitchen downstairs. I think he felt my impatience, my reluctance sometimes to welcome him into my life.

Sometimes I saw him waiting at the window in the evening, his old yet youthful face curious to see who would be dropping me home. Occasionally as I had lunch with my colleagues, laughing over a pint at the pub, I would think of his cheery face as he would bring out the lunches from the fridge, when we had sat together as a couple in front of Neighbours. I quickly brushed the memories away, so new and yet beginning to be unwelcome. We never had lunch together again.

The following month I packed my bags and prepared to leave. I bought Cecilia a rug for the living room with the money I had earned from my teaching, for Martin I bought a book about Indian literature. They both looked at me kindly, unable to say much. Recently I had often come home to find they had both gone to bed. The summer evenings were still long and yet they seemed to find solace in the darkness of their room. I heard Cecilia crying one night, her eyes looked blue and puffy as she came down the following morning. Another night I heard their whispers, the bed creaking, her moans of pleasure. I smiled at that, I could feel their warmth through the wall, their togetherness.

They gave me a small radio, like the one I had in the room upstairs which I had enjoyed listening to so much. I was grateful for this, it would be the only electronic device I owned to begin my life at Oxford. Martin helped me load my luggage in the back of the car and took me to the station. He smiled at me, his eyes dark and moist, the September sun setting behind him, mellow and golden tinged with pink like a myriad of flamingos settling around us. He held me against him and I could feel him trembling. I felt sorry to leave him behind, he had after all made me welcome, made me forget about loneliness in an alien land. He suddenly looked his seventy years; his face puckered and creased; his lips dry and quivering.

"Thank you Indira." he whispered. "Thank you for bringing me sunshine."

I turned to go, my train awaited me, Oxford and its gleaming spires awaited me. In a few weeks he would be forgotten, an anecdote to be retold to friends over a glass of Scrumpy, and a few laughs. Perhaps I would revisit him in a few years, but I knew for sure that things would have changed by then and once again all I took with me were a few reluctant memories of a place I once called home. I think he sensed this as he left for his home up that crooked hill, on that unchanging stretch of road to a wife who smiled at him through the net curtains.

A Perfect Match

The gift of a slim, leather-bound book of Tagore's poetry was what finally made Sushima look up and smile.

So far, sitting in one corner of the living room, she had been indifferent. Many prospective suitors had been to see Sushima over the past few months, and she did not expect the retired Doctor and his son Mahesh to be distinct from the rest. That was of course until the Doctor handed her the book. Later, the Lahiri household would be in awe over this simple act. Not so much because of the Doctor's kindness, but the fact that anyone could be liberal enough to think of offering his potential daughter-in-law such a gift. Immediately, he was perceived as a man of vision, of class and impeccable sophistication. Unlike that which most visitors brought along, it was not just a regular box of *mishti* from the best known sweet shop in town, or a packet of the spiciest mix of *chanachur*, but a book of Tagore's finest poetry. Even Sushima had to agree that the man had style.

Later that evening Sushima looked through the poems in the book. She thought of her future father-in-law's kind features, his long sloping forehead, the greying temples which gave him such a distinguished air. Her parents had agreed to the match almost immediately after the book was handed to her. Of course, they hadn't asked her consent. Sushima knew that asking her consent was not customary, but nevertheless they were pleased to observe her acquiescence. Anyone could have seen that in her smile, the slight nod of her head as she bent down to touch the Doctor's feet.

A few months ago Sushima had been reluctant to entertain any thoughts of marriage. Unlike most Bengali parents, the Lahiri's were not severe in their expectations of their four daughters. But Mr Lahiri had recently fallen upon hard times, his once thriving business of luxury leather goods, had slowly diminished as demands for synthetic materials consumed the public.

Sushima knew that with her degree from the local college she had no great career prospects. Briefly she had thought about getting a job, perhaps teaching at the local school or as a salesgirl in one of the upcoming department stores in town. This would only be a temporary solution though, and she knew that her meagre income would not help take the stress off her parents' shoulders.

She was the youngest of the four sisters. Her three elder sisters had been successfully married off over the last couple of years. It was lonely in the large house without them, and Sushima eagerly awaited their visits. They came laden with gifts for their parents and youngest sister, and for a few days the otherwise quiet house would come alive with their infectious happiness. Most of all, Sushima looked forward to the mischievous stories they had to share about their husbands; to the laughter and giggles that consumed the sisters under the shadows of their mosquito net at night.

When she finally agreed to marry, Sushima's parents hastily put out an advertisement in both the local English and Bengali newspapers.

Beautiful, fair, Brahmin Girl. 21 years old, English speaking. Welcomes prospective grooms with good educational qualifications. Business man acceptable. Please send Bio data and photograph.

Consequently there followed a number of eligible and some not-so-eligible suitors. Sushima would spend long afternoons sprawled across the large four-poster bed in her parents' room, going through each letter and photograph with her mother. At first Sushima was curious to see what she was bargaining for. Mostly the letters that accompanied the small photographs were full of accolades for the perfect man. They all sounded the same to her, excellent job prospects, very good-looking, tolerant, perfectly fluent in three or four languages. She began to wonder if any of them had even the slightest semblance of honesty or modesty about them. It made her uncomfortable to think of them, and quite often when they did meet, she found them arrogant and self-centred.

So when Sushima saw the Polaroid photograph of Mahendra along with the letter of introduction from his father she barely spared it a glance, expecting the same story as she had already read several times before. Her mother picked it up and read through it quietly, after which she turned and smiled at Sushima.

"This is the one Sushima; this is the perfect match for you".

She read aloud from the letter,

"Father and son live alone, mother died years ago, father is a retired Doctor, and the son is studying for his Engineering final exams". She put the letter and photograph down and beamed at her daughter as if she had at long last found the hidden treasure,

"Just imagine, no mother-in-law to meddle with you, no jealous sparring sisters-in-law, no loafer brother-in-laws? Its perfect!" she exclaimed, now excited at the prospect.

Sushima thought how callous her mother's words sounded; how she appeared almost joyous at knowing that the boy had grown up without a mother, the father without a wife. But heartless as it did sound, she knew her mother was right. The household sounded uncomplicated, a perfect match indeed.

Mahendra's father the Doctor was contacted. Letters were exchanged as well as a rather inhibited photograph of Sushima. And so it was that on the day that Doctor Basu and his son Mahendra came to meet Sushima and her family, she was beguiled with the gift of the book of poetry. Later that night, lying awake within the pink gauze of her nylon mosquito net, it occurred to her that she had hardly noticed Mahendra. Vaguely she recalled a fair face looking down upon sandaled feet, hair dark but thinning on an egg-shaped forehead. He had sat almost unnoticed, barely speaking unless spoken to. Everyone in the room had just been attentive to the father. He spoke for his son, his voice gentle and refined, and his laughter warm and yet controlled like a well tuned musical instrument. Sushima had caught her mother staring at the Doctor in awe, and she knew what she must have been thinking: how cultured and educated he was next to her own rather unsophisticated and loud husband.

When Sushima was called in to the living room as was customary he had looked at her appreciatively. She stood by the door as if to escape at the first opportunity, and only once had she looked up at him to see his smiling eyes behind his dark-rimmed glasses, the precious folds of his starched white dhoti as they formed a fan against the armchair where he sat.

"Do you sing *Ma?*" he had asked her gently, addressing her in the customary respectful way as mother. She had nodded.

"She is an expert in all kinds of *Rabindra Sangeet,*" added Gauri looking encouragingly at her daughter.

"Go on dear, why don't you sing something for the Doctor." Urged by her mother she had sung, her voice high yet uninhibited the words rolled over her tongue onto the whitewashed walls and then floated up into the palm trees that swung over the green pond next to the house. It was not an exceptional voice but pleasing enough to the ear and the Doctor looked impressed at the end and immediately asked for an encore. He nodded at his son who was looking out of the windows at the maid who was taking the washing to the *ghat.*

"*Ki* Mahendra?" he asked his son, who as soon as he was addressed looked down at his shoes again.

"Wasn't that great?" he reiterated. Mahendra mumbled something in response, whilst everyone waited quietly, not sure of what to say, or whether to wait for a clearer answer. The Doctor diverted everyone's attention away from him by asking for more.

As the wedding day approached there was jubilation in the house, after all a perfect match had been found for the youngest daughter. An auspicious day had been fixed, when the moon was in perfect alignment with the earth. In fact Doctor Basu had insisted on the very first date on the calendar. No wasting time when a match is so perfect he had said. Of course by then everyone in the household was so enamoured with Sushima's future father-in-law that his word was taken as the law.

The house was whitewashed for the occasion. A motley group of painters came and splashed fresh paint outside and inside the house. For a while the damp acrid smell of whitewash enveloped everything, from their clothes to the food they ate, but eventually when the cooking began the week before the wedding it dissipated into the smell of the frying fish and the vegetables and the dry cooked mutton.

Sushima was a trifle lonely that week. Her sisters had come to stay but they had taken a matronly interest in the wedding arrangements having experienced it not so long ago themselves. So Sushima sat for hours by herself on the roof thinking of the life ahead of her, the house she was going to and her father-in-law the retired Doctor. She rarely thought of Mahendra, somehow after seeing him that once he had not left a lasting impression on her, but she reassured herself that she would have plenty of time to get to know him.

Occasionally she let her mind wander to thoughts of his hands touching her in the dark, a room which she drew out of her imagination, and hands that could have belonged to anybody. There was no face above her, it was dark and in the softness of a winter afternoon lying down on the roof she let herself feel the ecstasy and tremor that the touch of her husband would incite in her. Her trips to the roof became more frequent, sometimes with the excuse of a few books she would lay next to the inner wall under the green canopy of the trees for the entire afternoon.

Her parents noticed her distracted air, the faint distance in her expression as she wandered absent-minded amongst the guests who had started to arrive a week before the actual wedding date.

As the day dawned there was a flurry of action in the household. Voices, both merry and frazzled carried across the rooms, workmen were still adding finishing touches to the marquee and huge baskets of flowers, orange marigolds and red roses and white heady-scented *rajnigandhas* were gathered together in bunches and hung from all the walls. Under the trees, the cooking had begun in earnest in enormous vats; the aroma's wafting across the lawn into the house.

From mid afternoon, after being anointed with turmeric, Sushima took her bath and began to get ready for the evening. Her sisters helped her put on her red and gold sari and then they carefully dotted sandalwood on her forehead. On her head they put over her veil a tiara made of fragrant white *rajnigandha*. Then they took her to the living room. As she sat in her splendour on a silk mat on the floor she heard the first strains of the *shehnai* as they struck up their woeful wedding tune. The groom's party had arrived and suddenly she found herself alone as everyone had fled to get a first glimpse of him. As Sushima sat by herself the first stirrings of nervousness tickled the insides of her belly, her toes twitched almost as if she was teetering on the edge of a cliff ready for a fall. She was tempted to get up and pace the room, peer out of the shutters to the lawn downstairs where all the commotion was. Perhaps she could get a better glimpse of Mahendra. Were his eyes brown or black, was his mouth a pout or a thin smirk? She wondered now in sudden alarm, at her lack of knowledge about this person that she was about to marry and spend the rest of her life with.

"Didi sit down, what are you doing up" said a distant young cousin who ran in panting with excitement,

"Your father-in-law is coming up to give his blessing. Quick, quick sit down again."

"Are they here?" Sushima asked awkwardly knowing fully well that they were. She gathered her red and gold sari under herself as she sat down again on the mat. Her cousin adjusted her red gauze veil around her face, the *rajnigandha* tiara upon her head slightly awry from all her pacing.

"Didi your *Shashur Moshai* looks so poised. Your mother was right; he really seems to be the perfect match"

Sushima was confused, was this perfect match that this young cousin spoke of so effusively Mahendra or his father? Panic gripped her throat, tightened the muscles momentarily as she tried to swallow, her breath coming inconsistently, her chest tight with fear.

A small group of people lurched into the room suddenly crowding around her so she felt small and vulnerable sitting on the floor. She saw the Doctor, uncharacteristically tense, his starched *dhoti* now rumpled like paper around his legs. He stood surrounded by people, eyes blinking behind dark-rimmed glasses. When he saw Sushima, sitting with her head down on her mat on the floor he composed himself and sat down in front of her. Everyone else followed suit and soon there were people leaning over her and around her, peering from over the Doctor's stooping shoulders as he fumbled in the pockets of his *Punjabi* for the carefully guarded gift he had brought for her. He took out a small cloth bag from which there emerged a solid gold necklace in three hanging layers, he held the edges and put it gently around Sushima's neck. He fumbled with the catch and she felt his fingers on the skin of her neck, warm and soft, a thinking-mans hands. She looked up momentarily into his eyes and the fear which she had felt all evening reached a crescendo that made her immobile. She hurriedly touched his feet and felt his hand upon her head in blessing.

On the lawn where the wedding ceremony was held, Mahendra stood with his back to Sushima as she was carried across on the traditional wooden slat by two sturdy cousins. Once she was brought around to face him she removed the green heart-shaped *paan* leaf from before her eyes to look at him. They looked into each others eyes for the first time as everyone cheered at this auspicious moment.

Sushima's first thought was how different Mahendra looked at such close quarters. He was actually rather good looking. His mouth was startlingly pink in an square face and although his hair was thinning it was parted in a boyish kind of way that lent him an unusual charm. He looked at her seriously, no smile played upon his lips, no hint of joy in his eyes, in fact Sushima wasn't even sure that he could see her, his eyes looked so distant and almost vacant. The ceremony continued to bind them together for a lifetime as husband and wife.

Later that night when all was over and the hundreds of guests had left after an evening of well fed entertainment, Sushima sat alone on her bed. The parting in her hair showed a blast of vermillion powder, like an erupting volcano in the middle of her head. She had changed out of her Banarasi sari and veil and had wiped the remnants of make-up off her face. Tonight she was to sleep with her sisters again. Mahendra was in the guest room on his own. The Doctor and a few other relatives from the Groom's side slept downstairs in the second reception. It was unusual for the Grooms parents to stay behind after the wedding ceremony but the Doctor had differed saying that they had come a long way and it would perhaps be better if they all travelled back home together the next morning. When Sushima found out from her elder sister that she would be leaving the following morning instead of at dusk as was traditional, she was slightly uneasy. She had looked forward to her last day at her parents house, the banter that often accompanied the day after the wedding ceremony was the highlight for most families as they relaxed and got to know the new couple. Instead she was being whisked off at dawn with a car load of strangers.

Her mother came in to see Sushima sitting on the bed absent-mindedly wrapping the end of her sari around her fingers.

"What's the matter Sushima?" she asked hesitantly, guessing instantly what must be on her daughter's mind. Her heart was heavy when she thought of saying farewell to her youngest and dearest child, but at least she knew that she was sending her to a good home, a good father-in-law who would look after her like his own daughter. She sat down on the bed next to her, her hips glad for the rest after the activities of the day. She looked tired, her once fair face had dark spots on the cheek bones and her chin showed signs of the stresses of the last few weeks.

"The ceremony went so well, your father and I are very relieved. The food turned out quite good too although I think there should have been more salt in the fish fry" she added looking at Sushima as she sat with her chin on her knee.

"Ma, why do we have to leave so early?" Sushima asked, sadness in her voice. She hesitated, looked at her daughter, her face powdered with spots of vermillion powder, her eyes marked with lines of kohl.

"Chandan Nagar is quite far you know. I think what the Doctor has suggested is quite sensible. After all he is a modern highly educated man, how does it matter if he breaks with tradition once for the sake of convenience and practicality? We should all learn from this, things can change we don't have to stick to rules, no?" She looked at Sushima waiting for her to concur with her explanation. Her daughter was silent for a few moments and then sighed gently in resignation.

"But Ma why do you have to agree with everything he says? You barely know him?"

The mother was taken aback by her daughter's response. Momentarily she looked confused then she put on a stern face and looked at her daughter,

"What do you mean barely know him? He is your father-in-law and you must obey all he says, full stop. Do not question his decisions, that will be the secret to your happiness in your husband's home. Look how well your sisters have adapted to their new homes, it's because they obey and agree, and I sincerely hope that you Sushima will do the same." She got up as she spoke and looked now quite crossly at her daughter.

"You must make him happy" she added. "Now get some sleep as the cars will leave at five in the morning." As she turned to go she felt sad to see her daughter look so melancholy, especially since she had been so convinced of her happiness over the last few weeks. She left Sushima thoughtful, still sitting on the bed, waiting for her sisters to join her, waiting for dawn when she would leave her home forever.

*

The house in Chandan Nagar was much smaller than she had imagined. Her parents who had visited it once in the weeks before the marriage had come back raving about this perfect house in the middle of the country with gardens that looked onto a lake.

"You will be so happy there" her mother had said and her father had nodded in agreement.

Now Sushima looked upon a single-storey bungalow with a small garden where there grew a pomegranate tree and a few tall beetle nut trees. It had all been a blur, the waking up in the morning, the journey into a part of Bengal where she had actually never been before.

*

She had looked at the back of the Doctor's neck all five hours across the city and beyond. The ride was bumpy and they stopped a few times for refreshments which she ate frugally. All the while Mahendra sat quietly in the seat next to her. An hour into the journey she heard a soft humming of the song she had sung when they had first met, that afternoon when the Doctor had given her the book. She glanced towards Mahendra and saw how he hung half his body out of the window and sang into the wind, his lips barely parted, unconscious of anyone near him or of the passers by who looked at this strange vision hurtling by over the streets of Bengal.

The car had been covered with flowers, and people were naturally curious to see what the bride and groom inside looked like. Whenever the car stopped they peered into the rear windows as Sushima sat with her red veil drawn low over her face. Catching a glimpse of the brides face was what everybody wanted and Sushima felt honoured and celebrated. Although she felt a closeness to all the strangers who looked into the car, her heart was heavy with the distance that increased between herself and her parents' home. The closer they got to her destination the more alone she felt, the more she wished she could see a familiar face amongst those who peered into the car.

In a small village close to Chandan Nagar, the cavalcade of wedding cars stopped near a cluster of shops. It was late afternoon now and people had started waking from their siesta, an aging Sadhu sat up beneath his tree and rubbed his eyes. A few stray dogs scratched and yelped needlessly at the cars until a few sharp pebbles thrown in their direction quietened them. A group of young boys, ranging from around nine to fifteen years of age walked across an adjoining paddy field laughing and chatting. They had obviously been for a swim as their naked torsos were wet and shining and their shorts and trousers clung dripping to their skin. As they saw the cars stopping under the trees they had quickened their pace, an innocent excitement at being able to see the bride and groom, sitting in cars that had obviously driven through the city.

The shopkeeper started handing out small glasses of steaming hot tea to the drivers and passengers. No one asked Sushima what she would like, her lips were parched, and she was desperate for some tea but too shy to ask. Her Father-in-law stood talking to one of the drivers in the shade of a tree. She was suddenly acutely conscious of Mahendra next to her, through the red gauze of her veil she felt his gaze upon her, and realised that this was the first time they had actually been left alone, as man and wife, sitting in the back of a flower bedecked Ambassador in the middle of nowhere. She felt him clear his throat, gently as if ready to say something to her, the singing of the past two hours had obviously hoarsened his voice, he must have caught all that dust in his throat, Sushima found herself wondering.

"Would you like some tea?" he rasped his voice almost ethereal in its anonymity. She smiled under her veil and gently nodded her head hoping that he would take that as a yes.

"Baba, says I must look after you" he added with a curiously boyish frankness. She trembled, happy that he wanted to do so. There were a few moments of silence before he opened the rickety car door and stepped out a few yards to the tea stall. She watched his back, in the white crumpled and sweaty kurta, the dhoti that wrapped in an ungainly fashion around his legs. He stood next to his father and spoke for a moment. He was shorter than his father, and as Sushima looked she felt a stirring of an almost maternal affection for him, for his eccentric singing, his quiet aloofness, and his awkward looks. She felt confused at her feelings, this was the kind of tug she felt when she played with young cousins, or once when she had found a puppy asleep under the stairs. Was this how she should be feeling now?

Momentarily she was distracted from her thoughts of Mahendra by the group of boys who had reached the cars and were clustered around, trying to get a look in at the bride. They smiled and giggled and shook their dark locks like a bunch of wet puppies after a swim. Sushima smiled to herself underneath her veil as they jostled each other to get a look at her.

Suddenly, she heard a shout and the boys jolted and scattered like a handful of peanuts. Sushima looked up and saw a red-faced Mahendra running towards the car. In one hand he had lifted up his dhoti until it reached his knees and in the other he held a glass of tea which was probably meant for Sushima. The boys ran in fear across the open area as Mahendra screamed at them to get away from the car, he kicked the dust with his sandaled feet, the tea splashed over his white clothes and he tore around like a rapid dog, eager to bite the people around him. His lips had lifted in a ferocious snarl and Sushima saw globules of spittle fly across the air landing in small craters on the dusty stretch.

Mahendra's father and a driver then stepped across and took hold of both his arms and dragged him to the car as he foamed and grunted under his breath. She could not hear what his father said to him, but his face looked stern and flustered. They bundled Mahendra back in next to her and she could feel his breath hot and steaming the inside of the car. The group of boys were now laughing and jeering at him, pointing to him, knowing he was out of reach and inside the car, knowing that they were safe to do and say whatever they liked. The driver got hurriedly back into his seat and her father-in-law climbed back in next to him wiping the back of his neck. Sushima thought she saw his hands tremble.

The rest of the journey was made in silence, the trees quiet, the landscape silent, and the inmates of that cavalcade of cars speechless until they arrived at the house. Sushima finally stepped out and considered her new home.

*

Sushima could not get the incident at the tea stall out of her mind. Mahendra's red face, the spit at the corners of his mouth, his bulging veined eyes as he screamed at the innocent boys. She wondered why he had reacted like that? Was this normal? Was it something she would have to get used to? There had been no explanations for his behaviour after the incident, just a nervous silence from her father-in-law. Mahendra fell asleep in the car, exhausted after his outburst, and waking up he treated her as before, a complete stranger. Those few moments they had exchanged in the car were lost forever.

Yet regardless of this ominous start, life in the house in Chandan Nagar settled into a routine. The house itself was small yet welcoming in a haphazard bachelor kind of way. There was a living room and three other rooms, one of which was her father-in-law's, the next Mahendra's which was now hers as well. The third room was rarely used but sometimes Sushima caught the Doctor sitting quietly in there. In the middle was an open dining area which led out to the kitchen.

One other inhabitant of the house was Binadi. The first time Sushima saw Binadi she balked. Binadi was an elderly lady who had been with the family ever since Doctor Basu was a child, which meant that she was actually older than the Doctor himself. She was born in Krishna Nagar which was now part of Bangladesh and had evacuated the country at partition. She had been a child and then a woman in their home and had even married and left them for a few years only to return a childless widow. Binadi had been only eleven when she had married and fifteen when she was widowed but she insisted on shaving her head as was the age old custom for widows, as well as to wear only a thin white cotton sari on her bare upper body.

Underneath her incredibly flat feet Binadi suffered from a multitude of calluses which she often sliced off with the sharp edges of a loose razor blade. Consequently she walked with a sliding, slithering movement along the cold floors whilst her arms hung back at an angle behind her almost touching her calves as she bent backwards at the waist. Her skin was hairless and papery, cracked in the sun and with age into a million wrinkles. When she smiled she showed two grey teeth that matched the hard stubble of her hair. But regardless of her almost corpse-like looks, Binadi was an integral part of the small household, and although she lived like a servant, sleeping on the floor in the kitchen and eating her huge mound of rice in the corner, her approval was sought when the new bride was brought into the house.

"So Monu found a pretty wife," she said, cackling as Sushima's veil was lifted by one of the many helpful neighbours wives who had come in to escort the bride and groom into the motherless household. She looked at Sushima smiling and then placed a gold coin in her palm. At first unsure of the elder woman's status, Sushima bent down to touch her feet, but Binadi quickly turned to Mahendra.

"Come Monu, have you eaten?" she abruptly moved her focus towards him almost as if Sushima was a disappearing apparition. Sushima noticed how Mahendra followed her into his room so that he could change. She knew there was bound to be an attachment between them, after all she was the one who had brought him up since Mahendra's mother had died.

Later that evening Sushima had showered in the dark, damp-smelling bathroom. It felt as if she had walked into a bachelor's living quarters. The soap in the bathroom was a medicinal Lifebuoy, not the sweet smelling variety which she had been used to growing up in a house with her sisters. The *gamcha's* and towels were damp and unaired and there was no dressing table or full-length mirror where she could check the pleats of her sari when she was ready. Mahendra's room which she was now to share had nothing but a bed with a blue mosquito net and a desk where she found piles of books which he was studying for his degree. There was a clothes horse in the corner which held a dishevelled array of his trousers and shirts and pyjamas. All Sushima's cases and belongings were shoved in a rather ungainly fashion underneath the bed. As they had sat down for the evening meal of rice and fish, Sushima had sensed her father-in-law watching her movements as she stood around serving him and Mahendra. They were awkward with this as until now it had only been Binadi sloshing things around as she slithered back and forth from the kitchen, cackling away under her breath. Nevertheless Sushima watched her husband and his father eat before she served herself.

"Sit with us and eat Sushima," he asked her gently but she smiled and continued serving. He let her carry on and addressed Mahendra,

"Monu, you must show Sushima around tomorrow. Today it is too late and dark and you both must be tired, but tomorrow you must show her the *pukur* and the fields that reach beyond. Also perhaps take a walk to your old school and college?"

Mahendra grunted and ignored his father and continued to eat. He shovelled the rice haphazardly into his mouth, and it fell messily around his plate whilst his hands were covered with the mixture, not just his fingertips as was usual. Sushima felt queasy. She looked at his hands, small and meaty, covered in the yellow specks of rice, the gravy oozing from between his fingers. Tonight she would share a bed with this man and those hands would be eager to reach out and touch her. The thought made her uneasy, not the eager anticipation she had dreamt of on the roof at her parent's home. Mahendra finished and left the table to wash.

"Baba," she addressed her father-in-law directly for the first time "would you like some more *daal?*" she saw him start as she addressed him, and he looked at her awkwardly as if he was desperately trying to say something. It was as if there was some secret which he wished to share, something that she ought to know, but he kept quiet and looked down at his plate and shook his head. After she had eaten her share of fish, rice and *daal* Sushima helped Binadi tidy up the kitchen. She put away the leftover food into pots and bowls which she fished out from the cockroach faeces- smelling cupboards. Binadi sat on her haunches washing the dishes, babbling away as Sushima worked. Already on this first evening together both women felt comfortable in each others company. Both knew that the other would be the only female company in this household.

"Monu is a good boy," Binadi said almost talking to herself "sometimes at school he used to play errant, this was after his mother died, poor dear." Binadi shook her stubbly head and sucked in her breath at this.

"So what if he has no friends? It is nothing strange; people talk and say funny things but you must not listen. He is a good soul and now you belong to this house like me you will soon learn to hold its secrets within yourself."

"What secrets Binadi?" Sushima could not help asking, intrigued.

"Oh nothing, nothing. Just don't let anyone tell you any old rubbish about our Monu. He is brilliant you know, first class first, gold medallist," she said with pride in her voice. Sushima looked down upon the shaven head and the gnarled hands that washed the dishes. What secret was it that she kept within herself and which Sushima would soon be obliged to find out? She had started to dread the unknown, having travelled this far on the basis of a perfect union she was not sure about handling any further surprises.

She had taken her time in the kitchen and then in the bathroom. She saw a crack of light shining from within her father-in-law's room as she walked past it, and wondered whether she should knock and wish him goodnight. Having brought her all this way, after the fanfare of the wedding, it suddenly seemed that she had always been here, these walls were not unfamiliar, the floors the ceiling, she had seen it all before. She decided not to knock after all.

Mahendra was asleep when she went to their room. The door creaked as she closed it behind herself, the two green shutters awkwardly misaligned. She wondered what she should do, whether she should lie down next to him or on the floor. A thought suddenly crossed her mind, what was she supposed to wear to bed? Her nightdress, a new one which her mother had carefully packed for her lay in a suitcase underneath the bed, dragging it out would cause too much noise. She did not want to wake him. She stood quietly in the shadows for what seemed like eternity, the moonlight filtered haphazardly through the shutters, making cold slashes across the bed where her husband lay. Momentarily she thought she would remove her clothes and go and lie next to him naked, this would please him and also save the trouble and dismay that she knew would come from fumbling with clothes in the dark. Her sisters had giggled one night about some such thing, the pleasure their men took if their women were forward. But Sushima was scared, too scared to move, she did not know him, all she had seen was his unreasonable rage. Finally, after two hours went by and she found herself tiring of standing in the corner she crept to the bed and gently lifted the mosquito net to lie next to him. She made sure that nothing of her person touched his. Later she turned her back to him and fell asleep.

*

The days fell into a routine. Sushima would often wake up to find Mahendra had already left the bed. She would usually find him on the roof with his books, pacing the cement from one end to the other, the tops of the *supari* trees lending their meagre shadows to his morning. He would have already bathed leaving his nightclothes strewn in wet puddles upon the bathroom floor which Sushima picked up and washed. Sushima seemed to barely make a change to his life, she was just an unnecessary accessory which his father had insisted he get, otherwise she lay unnoticed spending most of her time with Binadi.

At night she lay awake anticipating his touch but it never came, he rarely turned over in his sleep which was as sound and dreamless as a new born babes. In the morning she woke up cold and untouched, he was already on the roof muttering away from his history book. It was then that Sushima began to question why she was here.

The Doctor went to the local hospital to support new staff three times a week. The rest of the days and the weekend he stayed at home and spent most of his time in his room reading or listening to music. Sushima found herself lingering closer to him, dusting the books in his room, or even sorting out his cupboard. She took him his tea on occasion and they would talk, mostly pleasantries, about home, about a visit from her parents and even about his college. On one such occasion as she came to his room with a tray of tea and biscuits she found it empty. Perhaps he had just gone to the bathroom. She put the tray down on a corner of his desk and as she rearranged a couple of open books to make space she noticed a black and white photograph underneath it all. She picked it up to look more carefully. It was the picture of a woman, in her early twenties, smiling straight into the camera, her beautiful face the perfect shape of a *paan* leaf, the eyes long and dark, the brows perfectly formed. There was something so familiar about her, something that Sushima knew she had seen somewhere before, perhaps not so long ago. A mole on her chin heightened the beauty of the face like a small point of affirmation.

"It's your mother-in-law," he had come up quietly behind her, as she looked at the photo. She turned around hastily, almost dropping the photograph. She felt his breath on her shoulders; saw the sadness of his smile as he took the photograph from her trembling hands. She wanted to tell him then that she understood his grief, his longing for his beautiful wife. Suddenly she felt she could not speak, the words constricting in her throat. She realised now what she had found familiar in the beautiful face. She had seen it once before, on her wedding day, as she had moved the *paan* leaf away and looked into her husband's same inexpressive eyes.

*

Mahendra never did take Sushima on a trip to visit the neighbourhood. She had never asked but often she found herself standing on the front veranda looking wistfully at the trees to what lay beyond. They had very few visitors, so Sushima's interaction with the outside world became very limited. Sometimes she yearned for the freedom she had known as an unmarried girl, the trips to the local market with her friends, jostling with people to buy bangles or eat *phuchka*. The furthest she had been here was to the well in the backyard. She had stood there one afternoon looking at their hollow green waters that seemed to echo each breath she took. She had dropped a small piece of slate inside, and waited for the echo of its splash to float up and reach her in the solitude of the afternoon.

One afternoon the Doctor suggested that she should accompany him on a walk. At first Sushima had hesitated, overcome with a sudden shyness even though she had spent the last hour discussing Tagore's *Monihara* with him. They often discussed Tagore, both of them had found a common passion in literature. She loved the way he spoke, so knowledgeably, and with such fervour. She had a sudden thirst for an education when she was with him. Her parents had not been very literary people themselves and Sushima realised that there had been so much lacking in her upbringing. After the incident with the photograph, Sushima and her father-in-law seemed to have crossed over a small threshold in a relationship which was desperate to flourish. In Tagore they found common ground; in his poetry, his music and his stories they found an excuse to come together.

Sushima hurriedly dressed herself in a blue silk sari with matching earrings and gold bangles that jangled on her wrist as she moved. As she stepped out of the house to where the Doctor waited for her she thought she caught a glimpse of admiration in his eyes. A glance that she had often seen him save for moments when he thought she could not see him. He walked beside her to the corner of the *pukur* where there was a small wall where one could lean over and watch the people at the different *ghats*. The water was a deep green and an early film of pond scum partially covered it where she knew there must be some fish eggs. She longed to dive into the water with free abandon as she had done when she was a child, swimming into the cool centre on a hot summer's day until she was just a headless being bobbing against the concentric ripple that she had made. But today she stood dressed like the newly wed that she was next to her father-in-law.

"Your mother-in-law loved this *pukur*" he said quietly. There was no passion in his voice, no affection, it was just a comment. Sushima thought of the picture of his wife; those dark, vacant eyes looking across the waters. She wondered whether she had felt the way Sushima felt now, at once thrilled to be in the company of this man, yet desperate to break free of the life she was leading.

"How did she die?" Sushima found herself asking suddenly. She did not know, because no one in the house ever spoke about her, including Binadi. He looked away thoughtfully, then turned to Sushima. She searched his face, the strong chin, the firm nose, the deep thoughtful eyes for an answer. She wanted to touch him, hold him against her own body in full view of all the passers by, all the people who were now doing their chores in the *pukur*. She suddenly did not care about the feelings that came surging to the surface of her mind.

"She drowned," he said "Here in this *pukur*."

Sushima was taken aback. She had never thought to ask until this moment but suddenly she wished she hadn't. He walked on ahead and she was unable to ask him much else for the rest of their walk. Once back home he took himself off to his room whilst Sushima changed out of her silk sari, though the bangles remained jangling on her hands all evening. After dinner in the kitchen she ventured to ask Binadi as she sat scraping the leftover *daal* and vegetables off their plates.

"Binadi, how did my mother-in-law die?" There was a pause in Binadi's enthusiastic scrubbing at the tap. She clicked her tongue a couple of times and looked back at Sushima, the milky whiteness of her left eye blinking sadly.

"She killed herself," she whispered, her voice catching the sound of the crickets as they orchestrated the darkness outside.

"What can I hide from you *Bouma*? You are now one of us" she began with a sigh, confirming to herself that it was fine to tell Sushima the truth.

"She went mad. She had this condition after she gave birth to Monu, which got worse and worse until she was a raving lunatic. It broke your father-in-law's heart to see her like that and he tried to keep it a secret as long as he could. He took her away for months on end to places where no one would know, no one asked any questions. But he had to come back, here to the house that he had built for her next to the *pukur* which she loved." She paused and looked carefully through the crack of the half open kitchen door to make sure that no one could hear her.

"She would often wake up at night screaming, tearing her clothes off and running into the streets. Then one day she woke up quieter than usual, left her husband and her son asleep in their beds and walked into the middle of the *pukur*. She couldn't swim, but she did not utter a cry or a scream to wake anyone. In the morning they found her washed up against the *ghat*, her body bloated and horrible."

Sushima stood gaping at all this, why had nobody ever mentioned this before? Was this why father and son remained so reclusive?

"Your father-in-law never forgave himself for not waking up and saving her from that last walk of hers. He is a raw and lonely man now, has been for years."

Sushima looked at Binadi, wondered how many other secrets and family tragedies this woman held within herself. What more did she know about her beloved Mahendra for example? Suddenly, Sushima realised why her husband refused to acknowledge her presence in the house and in their bed. He was his mother's son.

After six weeks of marriage Sushima had began to figure that Mahendra could not be normal. He barely spoke to her or anybody else in the house and yet she often caught him muttering to himself on the roof or on the front veranda. Binadi was the only one who approached him to ask him to come to dinner or lunch otherwise he wandered sullenly around the house.

One afternoon whilst the Doctor was out, Mahendra rushed outside to watch a man in the street showing off a monkey who could do tricks. Sushima looked through one of the windows as her husband stood amongst a crowd of children in the street, his pyjamas sagging so that she could see the upper ridge of his buttocks. The children noticed this and began to titter amongst themselves, ignoring the antics of the little monkey. Mahendra looked at them and let out a scream so that the children scattered away in fear and the monkey disappeared chattering inside its master's bag. Sushima hurriedly went into the kitchen to avoid confronting him when he came back indoors, angry and fuming.

"Blasted monkey, blasted monkey children," he muttered over and over again under his breath until Binadi came out and took him to his room to help him calm down. As the days went by, Sushima found herself angry at her father-in-law, at his deception, at her failed position as a wife. Who was she in this house? Why was she brought here with such fanfare? He had betrayed the trust of her parents and herself, in her heart she found this deed unforgivable yet she sympathised with his loneliness, his need for her company.

*

When Sushima went back to her parent's house for the first time since she had been married there was naturally a gush of excitement on her arrival. Her parents and sisters surrounded her after she alighted from the car commenting on how well she looked, how perfectly she suited the marital glamour. Sushima looked around herself at those beloved faces and wondered whether they could not tell in the least how miserable and scared and confused she was and how she had to spend her nights lying next to a madman.

After a meal that consisted of all her favourite food Sushima was whisked off by her sisters to answer all their curious questions about her new household. She noticed that one of her sisters was pregnant, her bump barely showing but her face had acquired a fleshy maternal glow.

"You are so lucky to be in charge of your own household," one sister began

"I have to listen to my mother-in-law and three demonic sisters-in-law. Your set up seems to be so perfect Sushima. You must feel quite spoilt?"

Sushima kept quiet and her sisters in their eagerness to discuss things mistook it for modesty. Later her mother came and lay next to them and there was a lot of merriment discussing their father's newfound passion for going to the market himself. Sushima sank into her old bed and wondered how distant she had become from all this, how unappealing it had seemed at times in the past but how golden and warm it seemed in contrast to her current life. And yet why was it that she felt a tug at her heart, a pining for something that she should rightfully be running away from?

Sushima left her parents with the impression of perfection which they had so mistakenly sent their youngest daughter to. She left her sisters giggling about Mahendra's prowess in the bedroom and how much bloom it had brought to her face, when they found her in moments of reverie they mistook it playfully for a new wife's yearning for her husbands embrace. After a week of such charades Sushima willingly left to go back to her home in Chandan Nagar. Although Mahendra would barely spare a thought for her, she knew her father-in-law missed her and she went back with the eager anticipation of his company.

Everything was exactly how she had left it, Mahendra pacing with his books on the roof, Binadi in the kitchen and her father-in-law waiting eagerly for his cups of tea. Sushima quietly slotted back into her role as if she had never left. She found it in herself to forgive the Doctor for his deception, for having cruelly snatched her away from the life she had led so far. There was a renewed tenderness in his actions towards her, ever since she had come back. It seemed as if they had finally understood that what lay between them was meant to be nurtured and moulded into something quite special, quite different to social expectations.

At night she slept next to Mahendra but during the day for all intents and purposes she fulfilled the role of companion to his father. No one noticed the exchanged looks between them the understanding and acknowledgements, the slight nods and gestures that were characteristic of a married couple.

In August Mahendra packed away his books and prepared to leave to take his examination. Binadi was quite distraught,

"How will my baby manage away in the big city for three nights. Perhaps you should go with him *Bouma*," she pleaded with Sushima.

But they all knew that this would not be possible. There was not really much he had to do except get to his destination which was a college in Calcutta and sit three consecutive days of exams. At night he would stay at the college guesthouse. Everything had been taken care of. A car had been hired to take him to the city and Sushima packed his suitcase carefully as he sat mutely upon the bed watching her like a child. He left with barely a glance at anyone.

That evening Binadi complained of a headache and retired early to her bed in the corner of the kitchen. Her father-in-law took out his record player and played some of his old *Rabindra Sangeet LPs*. Sushima brought out two cups of tea and sat on the floor at his feet, her head resting gently against his *dhoti*-clad knee. She felt his hand rest upon her head and the warmth that flowed through her from his touch. As the haunting melodies wrapped the small house together Sushima stood up to leave as he reclined on his easy chair, eyes closed. He took Sushima's hand in his and opened his eyes to look at her.

"I am sorry," he mouthed to her, and her eyes filled with tears as she watched him, the soundless tears which rolled down his cheeks like tiny rivulets.

That night as she lay alone on her bed and the distant music faded away and the night played its own hushed tune she closed her eyes and imagined herself alone on the rooftop before her perfect match was made.

Acknowledgements

T hank you to Sarah Savitt whose initial enthusiasm for my stories encouraged me to put together this collection. Her suggestions on the first draft remain invaluable and the warmth and generosity of her friendship have been vital to my literary output. And most of all, a special thank you to Sudipto Banerji, best friend, husband and unfaltering champion of my work.

Amongst Other Things, is a work of fiction. Events, characters and place names are purely a product of the author's imagination. If real, these are not portrayed with geographical and historical accuracy.

The following stories have been previously published: "Mrs Luthra's Stove" in *MsLexia* Issue 54 Jun/Jul/Aug 2012; "The Chair" in *Wasafiri* Issue 67, Autumn 2011; "Jamun Reverie" in *The Little Magazine* Volume 3 Issue 1, Family, 2002.